NO TIME FOR DOUBLE-TALK

Fritz and Hugo marched the Hardy boys down the corridor.

"I wonder what's waiting for us," Joe said to Frank as they walked along.

"I have a strong hunch that they have a big surprise in store," replied Frank. There was an odd mocking tone in Frank's voice, but Joe didn't have time to wonder about it.

"In there," said Hugo from behind.

As they entered the room, Frank said in the same strange tone, "Hi, Joe."

"Hi, Frank," answered the young man waiting inside.

Joe looked into the face of that young man—and suddenly wondered if he had really come out of his drugged trance, or if maybe he was as crazy as the inmates at the Lazarus Clinic used to be.

The young man he was staring at was himself!

Books in THE HARDY BOYS CASEFILES® Series

Available from ARCHWAY Paperbacks

THE LAZARUS PLOT

FRANKLIN W. DIXON

AN ARCHWAY PAPERBACK
Published by POCKET BOOKS
New York   London   Toronto   Sydney   Tokyo

AN ARCHWAY PAPERBACK *Original*

An Archway Paperback published by
POCKET BOOKS, a division of Simon & Schuster Inc.
1230 Avenue of the Americas, New York, NY 10020

Copyright © 1987 by Simon & Schuster Inc.
Cover art copyright © 1987 Brian Kotzky
Produced by Mega-Books of New York, Inc.

ISBN: 0-671-68048-X

First Archway Paperback printing June 1987

10 9 8 7 6 5 4

THE HARDY BOYS, AN ARCHWAY PAPERBACK and colophon are registered trademarks of Simon & Schuster Inc.

THE HARDY BOYS CASEFILES is a trademark of Simon & Schuster Inc.

Printed in the U.S.A.

IL 7+

THE LAZARUS PLOT

Chapter

1

"GOT YOU!" FRANK HARDY smiled grimly. Once again, the older of the two Hardy boys had made a capture. In this case, the capture was a fish.

Rushing water came up to the top of his hip-high boots as he braced himself against the current of the Allagash River. Above the tall pines on both banks of the river, the early fall sky was a dazzling blue. Frank felt a million miles away from the world of crime fighting and danger in which he and his brother, Joe, lived—and had nearly died. The fanatic followers of the Rajah and his *Cult of Crime* had done their best to fit Frank and Joe for matching coffins.

The Hardys had survived, however, and decided that a vacation was definitely in order. They'd packed their fishing and camping gear into

Joe's latest pride and joy, a 1958 station wagon complete with wood paneling, which he'd lovingly reconditioned. Next stop, the Maine north woods, for two weeks of peace, quiet, and fishing.

"Whoa, big fella," Frank muttered as his fishing rod began to bend. He let out some line as the fish fought to escape. From the feel of the line, the fish was a big one. Then he saw it leap into the air—a trout!

Just the right kind of adventure, he thought. Trout give you a challenge, put up a fight, and don't carry guns.

He fought the fish on his hook, letting out the line, then reeling it in, bringing the fish ever closer to his net. Already, he could picture it grilling over the campfire.

This is just what we need, he thought. Two weeks without having to look over our shoulders. Two weeks without racing against time to head off some disaster. Two weeks without mayhem, mystery, or murder. He grinned to himself. But will Joe be able to last two weeks without girls to chase?

His smile faded as he thought about Joe, back in town buying supplies. Frank had always kidded his brother about belonging to the "Girl-of-the-Week Club." But he knew that Joe had really and truly loved only one girl—Iola Morton. Then terrorists had bombed the Hardys' car, and Iola had disappeared in a fireball. It looked as if Joe

2

was never going to get serious about another girl again.

Would he ever get over it, Frank wondered, or would he be haunted by Iola's memory forever? Crashing noises from the nearby forest brought Frank whirling away from the riverbank. He turned just in time to see Joe Hardy tearing through the underbrush.

Frank shook his head. "You made me lose a fish," he complained. Then he saw his brother's face. "What's wrong? You look like you saw a ghost."

"I did," Joe said, still gasping for breath. *"Iola."*

"That's impossible," Frank said patiently. "Your mind is playing tricks. Iola's *gone,* Joe." Frank began to get worried. Had too much hardball with the bad guys scrambled Joe's brains?

"I know what I saw," Joe said, stubbornly shaking his head. "I left the car and was heading back here through the woods. And suddenly she stepped out from behind a tree less than ten yards from me. I saw her face as clear as day. She was wearing a sweater and jeans, just like the ones she was wearing before . . . before . . ." Joe's voice trailed off.

"You've got to face what happened," Frank said, putting his hand on Joe's shoulder. "Nothing was left of the car but a few hunks of molten metal after that bomb went off. There's no chance that Iola could have survived."

"But remember: *They didn't find a trace of Iola's body*," said Joe.

Frank saw the gleam of hope in Joe's eye. A crazy gleam, Frank thought, for a crazy hope.

"The police said the heat was so intense that it left no traces of her," Frank reminded him gently. "Except in your memory, Joe."

Joe's face tightened. "That wasn't a memory I just saw. It was *her*, as real as you or me."

"But did she say anything or do anything to make contact with you?" Frank asked. "The real Iola would have."

"She was about to say something," Joe said. "She saw me and opened her mouth to speak. Then all of a sudden she looked confused, like she didn't know where she was or what she was doing. Her eyes went blank, and she turned and ran. Before I could move, she'd disappeared in the forest."

"Vanished—just like that," said Frank skeptically.

"I don't care if you believe me or not. That's what happened," said Joe, now openly angry. "When I couldn't find her, I came back here to get you to help track her. She needs help, Frank. And if you won't help her, I'll have to do it alone."

He turned away from his brother and strode back into the forest.

"Joe! Wait!" said Frank, hurrying after him. "Stranger things than this have happened and turned out to be real. I'll come along if you want me to."

Joe flashed a smile at his brother. "I figured you wouldn't be able to resist a mystery. Come on, Sherlock. Together, we'll be able to pick up her trail."

"How will you find the spot where you first saw her?" Frank asked as they made their way through the forest. Sunlight filtering through the branches dappled the ground. The only sounds were the crunching of pine needles under the Hardys' feet, the buzzing of insects, and the occasional call of a bird.

"I dropped my pack with the supplies when I saw her, so it should still be lying there," said Joe. He squinted through the trees. "There it is now."

They stood beside the discarded pack.

"So where did this girl . . . Iola . . . come from?" Frank asked—and then he heard it.

Just a small sound.

A twig snapping, maybe, or pine needles crunching.

But it was a sound that somehow didn't belong, that made him want to dive for cover. Frank got a hold on himself, smiling at how on edge his nerves were. They were safe in the woods.

But Joe didn't think so. He grabbed Frank's arm and dived to the ground, dragging Frank with him.

"Joe—" Frank began, but a much louder sound drowned out his words.

Rifle shots exploded.

Bullets whizzed inches over their heads.

"It's a trap," Joe rasped. "And we're sitting ducks!"

Chapter

2

"GOT TO FIND cover," Frank whispered into his brother's ear as they lay side by side, facedown, hugging the ground. There were more rifle shots, more bullets whizzing above them.

"Good thinking," said Joe, already starting to roll himself along the ground toward the nearest large pine.

Frank followed him. They reached the side of the tree away from where the shooting was coming, and cautiously raised themselves to their hands and knees.

More shots. A bullet thumped into the tree, and another ricocheted off it, showering splinters of bark.

The Hardy boys hit the ground again. Wiggling on their stomachs, using their elbows to propel

7

them, they retreated farther away from whoever was using them for target practice.

The rifle shots ended. As Frank strained to cover ground, he kept his ears wide open for sounds of pursuit. But he heard none. Just the sound of Joe and him going over the blanket of pine needles, and the sound of their increasingly heavy breathing as their lungs began to burn.

Finally, it seemed safe to stop.

Concealed behind thick undergrowth, they again raised themselves to their hands and knees.

With the back of his hand Frank wiped away the sweat coating his forehead.

"Whew, close call," he whispered.

"Hey, remember what you told me about this trip?" Joe whispered back.

"No. What?" said Frank.

"'No bad guys, just good times,'" said Joe.

Frank shrugged. "Okay, so I was wrong." He edged his face toward a gap in the undergrowth to peer into the forest. "Looks like they're not coming after us."

"Then it's time for us to go after them," said Joe. His eyes were flashing like warning lights. People taking potshots at him triggered his temper.

Frank didn't have Joe's hot temper. Instead he had cool-headed logic. But he did share his brother's dislike of running from a fight—and Joe's determination to come out on top no matter what the odds.

8

"From the number of shots, it's a good bet there's more than one guy," Frank said. "We can't go straight at them, because it won't do any good to go charging into the barrels of their guns."

"We'll make a circle and approach them from behind," said Joe.

"Just what I was thinking," replied Frank. "And it would be even better if we split up. It'll double our chances of spotting them. If one of us does, he can give a signal. How about this?" Frank pursed his lips and whistled a whippoorwill call.

Joe replied with one of his own.

"It'll do," said Frank, nodding. We'll gamble that our pals out there won't know that whippoorwills do their calling at night."

"We won't even give them the time to think about it," said Joe. "We'll make sure they never know what hit them."

"We'll have surprise on our side," Frank agreed. "They'll never figure that we're coming after them." Frank checked the compass on his watch, and Joe did the same. "Okay. You go five hundred paces to the southwest. I go the same distance southeast. Then we trade directions, so we meet in another five hundred paces—unless one of us makes a sighting first."

"Catch you later," said Joe. He moved off, quiet as a cat, his expression alert and intent, like a tiger on the prowl.

Frank was just as alert. As he moved silently through the forest, he did a mental check on himself, as his karate teacher, Kim Sung, had told him to do in the moments before possible combat. He made sure his breathing was smooth and deep, his muscles relaxed and supple, his heartbeat slow and steady. That done, he went into the final stage of readiness, wiping all thoughts from his mind, so that his senses of sight, hearing, and smell would be clear and he could instantly react to danger.

Then he saw it—the glint of sunlight striking metal.

He knew what that metal was. It was the metal of a rifle.

Frank pursed his mouth to whistle, but it was too late.

A man stepped out from behind a tree. He was big, bald, and black bearded, over six feet tall and a good two hundred pounds. He looked like he had been outfitted from head to toe by L. L. Bean, complete with red-and-black-checked flannel shirt and hunting cap. But Frank barely noticed what the man looked like. All he was interested in was the rifle in the man's hands, pointed straight at him.

Frank had only a split second to make his move—and he made it. He stepped toward the man, raising his hands in surrender.

Then, without a break in movement, his leg shot upward, the tip of his boot catching the man square on the chin. The instant Frank felt his boot make solid contact, he twirled to one side, away from the rifle. His flow was perfect. Kim Sung would have been pleased.

The rifle dropped from the bearded man's hands as the man went down as if pole-axed, right into a thick patch of wild blueberries.

Direct hit, thought Frank—and that was his mistake.

Too late he remembered another of Kim Sung's teachings. Never let success distract you. Never congratulate yourself on doing well, because when you do that, you relax your guard.

Too late Frank realized someone had come up behind him. He only had time to half-turn before he saw the face of an angry man, his hands high above his head, and then the blurred shape of something—a rifle barrel, perhaps—coming down.

Then there was a sharp pain, and blackness.

Joe, moving silently through the forest, heard a crashing noise.

It might have been an animal running through the undergrowth.

On the other hand, it might have been a body falling to the ground.

Joe headed in the direction of the sound. He watched every step he took and kept close to every tree he went by.

After a moment, he heard voices and headed

toward them. The voices became more and more distinct, but he couldn't understand a word.

A foreign language, he thought as he pressed against a thick tree, then peered around it.

He saw two men—a big, bald, bearded one, with hands bleeding from some kind of scratches, and a wiry, redheaded one—standing over a body on the ground.

Joe recognized the body at the same time that he recognized the language the men were speaking.

It was Frank who was lying on the ground.

And it was French the men were speaking.

Were the men survivors of the French gang that the Hardy boys had broken up in their case *Evil, Inc.?* Were they out for revenge?

Joe let out his breath in relief when he saw Frank's head make a slight movement, his body give a tiny twitch. At least Frank was still alive.

The bearded man grinned. While the other man kept his rifle trained on Frank, the bearded man unhooked a canteen from his belt and poured water from it onto Frank's face.

Frank shook his head as he opened his eyes. Then the bearded man leaned down, grabbed Frank by the arm, and lifted him to his feet like a limp doll. When he let go, Frank stood there, weaving groggily, like a battered fighter set up for a knock-out punch.

As Joe grimaced in horror, he saw the wiry man get set to deliver it.

The man parted his lips in a snarl, lifted his rifle, and pressed the tip of the barrel against Frank's head, just behind his ear.

Joe could wait no longer. He moved out from behind the tree and charged.

He had never moved faster in his life—not on the football field going for a touchdown, not on the baseball diamond stretching a single into a double, not on a track heading for the tape in his specialty, the hundred-yard dash.

But even as his knees pumped and his feet flew faster and faster, he knew he couldn't reach Frank in time.

At the first crunch of Joe's feet on the pine needles, the wiry man wheeled around and leveled his gun at Joe.

This was one race Joe couldn't win.

He couldn't move faster than a bullet.

All Joe could do was brace himself to die.

Chapter

3

JOE DID NOT hear the rifle shot he was expecting. He did not feel a bullet slam into him.

Instead he heard the wiry man with the rifle gasp, "Aghhh!" as Frank karate-chopped him on one forearm, then the other, in a blur of motion. The rifle dropped from the man's paralyzed hands, and the man dropped on top of it, after Frank chopped at the back of his neck.

The bearded man reached for the hunting knife on his belt, but he never made it. Joe hit him in a flying tackle, smashing him back against a tree, then let him go and backed off a step. When the bearded man reached for his knife again, Joe lashed a right hook to the jaw. The man went down like a sack of flour.

"Good work," said Frank as he removed the

wiry man's belt and set about tying his hands behind his back with it.

"Good work yourself," said Joe, doing the same thing to the bearded man. "I thought I was a goner. I thought you were, too. You woke up in the nick of time."

"Actually, I came to a couple of minutes before, but I didn't see any sense in letting those guys know it," said Frank, squatting as he made sure the wiry man was securely tied. Then he stood up.

"Playing possum, huh?" said Joe, giving his man a final check and standing up, too.

"Right," said Frank. "I figured it might be interesting to hear what they had to say to each other when they thought I was unconscious. And of course, it would be a lot easier to make my move when their guard was down."

"Did they say anything?" asked Joe.

"Yeah, but I didn't understand what," said Frank.

"They were speaking French, I think," said Joe. "You must have understood *something*, unless that A you got in French class last year was a joke."

"I just caught a stray word here and there," said Frank, shaking his head. "They were speaking with some kind of weird accent. Plus they were talking real fast, and my head was still ringing, so it all sounded like Greek to me."

Joe laughed, then became serious. "We'll just have to wait until they come to before we find out what they're up to."

"We can speed up the process," said Frank, unhooking his canteen from his belt. "I'll do to them what they did to me—give them a water cure."

A minute later, the men were standing on their feet, shaking their heads.

"*Sacre bleu, qu'est-ce qui s'est passé?*" mumbled one.

"*Ma pauvre tête,*" groaned the other.

"Either of you speak English?" asked Frank.

"Yes, of course," the bearded man said with a heavy accent.

"Certainly," replied the other one, with a similar accent. "We come from Quebec. We French-Canadians must speak both French and English."

"Then you can start talking," said Joe, in a hard voice.

"Why were you taking target practice on us?" said Frank.

"On *you?*" said the bearded man. "Why should we shoot at you?"

"Think hard," said Joe, raising his fist menacingly. "You should be able to remember. It was just about fifteen minutes ago."

"*Mais non,* that was *you?*" said the wiry man. He turned to his companion. "I told you that you were mistaken when you said you saw deer. You are always so quick on the trigger."

"When you hunt, you must react instantly," said the bearded man defensively. "Otherwise, the deer, they get away. I saw the motion, I was sure it was the deer. Needless to say, I apologize."

"I must apologize, too, for hitting you over the head," the wiry man said to Frank. "But when I saw you attacking my friend Henri here, I had no choice. Who knew what kind of criminal or madman you might have been?"

"Jacques had to do it," Henri agreed. "After all, you attacked me without any reason."

"That gun you pointed at me seemed like reason enough," said Frank.

"I heard you coming through the undergrowth, and naturally I thought you were a—"

"Don't tell me—a deer," said Frank. "Listen, before I untie you, promise you won't make any more little mistakes. The woods aren't safe with trigger-happy hunters like you around—especially before the season officially starts." Smiling grimly, he took the bullets out of the rifle he was holding, picked up the other rifle and emptied it, then frisked the men, removing all the bullets from their pockets. Meanwhile, Joe searched their backpacks, which were lying nearby, and removed the rest of the ammunition from them.

"I suggest the two of you try fishing this time of year. It's safer for everyone concerned," said Frank as he and Joe untied the belts from Henri's and Jacques's wrists.

17

"You cannot do this," said Henri indignantly as he rubbed circulation back into his hands.

"It is outrageous," agreed Jacques.

But they took a look at Frank's hands spreading flat in readiness for another karate chop, and Joe's hands balling into fists, and limited further protest to Henri's saying, "You have not heard the last of this."

"We will notify the authorities," said Jacques.

"You do that," said Joe.

"Yeah, please," said Frank. "Once they hear our side of the story, you guys can forget about hunting again, unless you want to do it without a license."

"Okay, okay," said Jacques. "Maybe we do lose our tempers a little. And maybe we were a little too quick on the trigger—especially Henri. I have to admit, it is not the first mistake he makes today. Less than an hour ago, he almost shoot at another person."

"I tell you, she look just like a deer," muttered Henri.

" 'She'?" Joe asked instantly. "You saw a *girl*, near here, a little while ago?"

"She is wandering around like a lost one," said Jacques. "I have no idea what she is doing here in the middle of the woods. Certainly she is not dressed for it. She is wearing new jeans and a pretty sweater, like she is at a school picnic."

"Jeans and a sweater," said Joe, trying to keep his voice calm. "Tell me, what did she look like?"

"A pretty girl, on the petite side, with a face like, how you say, a pixie, and dark hair," said Jacques.

"Yes, dark hair, like an elk," said Henri.

"But you didn't shoot at her?" said Joe.

"No, of course not," said Henri.

"I grab his rifle just in time," said Jacques. "Then I call out to the girl. I think maybe she needs help. But when she hear me, she turn and run."

"Which direction?" asked Joe urgently.

"That way," said Jacques, pointing.

"Come on," Joe said to Frank. Without waiting for a response, Joe jogged off in the direction that Jacques had indicated, toward an opening in the trees and thick foliage.

"So long," Frank said over his shoulder to the two men as he followed his brother.

"Looks like we're on some kind of abandoned trail or road," said Joe as he jogged along at Frank's side.

"A road to nowhere," commented Frank. "It hasn't been used in years."

"Yes, it has—by that girl," said Joe, keeping up a fast pace until he halted abruptly. He picked a scrap of torn blue woolen material from the branch of a sapling where it had snagged. "I'd know this blue anywhere. It's the same color as the sweater Iola was wearing when I saw her before—and the last time I saw her, when . . ." Joe trailed off, wincing at the memory. Then his

19

voice grew urgent. "Let's speed it up! We're on her trail."

"But we're coming to a dead end," said Frank, peering ahead.

A hundred yards down the overgrown road was a tall wire fence topped by barbed wire. On a gate in the fence was a large sign. The Hardy boys were too far away to read the lettering, but they could make out the picture on it. A skull. The universal symbol of death.

When they reached the fence, Frank read: "Warning. Electrified fence. Property patrolled by armed guards and attack dogs. Trespassers will be shot on sight."

Joe refused to let that stop him. "Iola must have gotten through this fence—or been *taken* through it—somehow. The only other place to go is deeper in the woods and I don't see why she'd do that. We've got to get in there." He reached for the gate latch.

Frank grabbed his arm. "Careful. The electric current might be on. And even if it isn't, you can bet it's locked."

"We have to get through it," said Joe, peering through the wire mesh. On the other side was what had once been a handsome lawn and garden, but had become a jungle of high green grass, tall weeds, and a rainbow of flowers gone wild.

"Well," said Frank reluctantly, "I see three options for getting in. We could get a ladder and go over it, but getting past the barbed wire on top would be tricky, and we would be sitting ducks if any guard spotted us. We could cut through the fence, but that would be hard with the current on, and any disturbance in it might set off alarms. That leaves one other way."

"Going *under* it," said Joe. "We could get a couple of shovels and tunnel through and have good cover at the same time."

"Tonight. When we have the cover of darkness," said Frank firmly. "But this is ridiculous, Joe."

"I hate to wait that long. Something might happen to Iola by then," said Joe.

"See any other choice?" asked Frank.

"You and your logic," replied Joe, shaking his head. "Once, just once, I'd like to see you go with gut feeling and not brains."

"I'd rather use my head and save our necks," said Frank. "Anyway, there aren't many other places in this forest to go. If someone went inside, they're still there. Come on." Frank sighed. "Let's get to the general store in the village and buy a couple of shovels. Big ones. We'll have to do some heavy digging tonight. And while we're at the store, we can do some digging there. We can find out if anyone knows anything about this property."

Two hours later, after a jog back to the station wagon and a drive to the village, the Hardy boys had gotten both the shovels and some information.

The storekeeper was a tall, lanky, gray-haired man, who was as close-mouthed as most of the citizens of Maine that the Hardy boys had met. But the sight of the money that Frank and Joe laid out for a pair of high-priced shovels warmed him enough to loosen his tongue when they asked him about the fence in the forest.

"Figure that must be the old Lazarus place," he said, counting the money twice, then ringing it up on his antique cash register.

"The Lazarus place?" Frank repeated.

"Fact is, they called it the Lazarus Clinic," said the storekeeper. "Folks around here, though, got a different name for it. Lazarus Loony Bin. Some fancy New York doctor opened it and had a lot of rich patients for a while—until the folks paying the bills got tired of seeing no results, and the place went out of business."

"What's it being used for now?" asked Frank.

"*Ain't* being used. Hasn't been for two, three years," said the storekeeper disdainfully. "Crazy place for a crazy house, in the middle of nowhere. Lost a bundle, that doctor did."

"Thanks for the information," said Joe. Then he said to Frank, "Time to move."

"Hey, mister, you're forgetting your shovel," said the storekeeper as Joe dashed for the door.

"I don't think I'll need it," said Joe.

"Well, mister, our policy is no refunds," said the storekeeper.

"Don't listen to my brother. We'll take them both," said Frank, picking up the two shovels and following Joe, who was already halfway out the door.

As soon as they were in the station wagon, Joe said, "If that place isn't operating, the electric current won't be turned on in the fence. There won't be armed guards or dogs. We can go right in with a pair of wire cutters, if the gate is even locked. No wonder Iola disappeared so fast. She must have gotten in easily."

"I'm not so sure," said Frank. "That fence seemed to be in awfully good repair, and that warning sign looked freshly painted."

"We'll see when we get there," replied Joe, pressing down on the accelerator.

Night had fallen and the stars were out in a moonless sky when the Hardy boys arrived at the fence again.

"Now we'll check this thing out," said Joe. Before Frank could argue, Joe splashed some water from his canteen onto the fence.

"See? No current," Joe said triumphantly. "We could have been inside hours ago and have caught up with Iola by now, if you weren't so cautious. Frank, you have to learn that sometimes you just have to go for it."

With that, Joe turned the handle on the gate and gave a shove. The gate swung open.

"Easy as pie," he said. "Let's find Iola now."

"Hey, slow down," said Frank. "Joe, if there's anybody inside at all, it *may* be some girl, but don't you know that it can't be Iola? Not after what happened. She's gone. You're just setting yourself up for . . ." Frank trailed off.

Joe wasn't listening to him. He was already moving through the overgrown garden, toward the dark shape of a massive building. Frank, shaking his head, had no choice but to catch up with his brother and try to keep alert to possible danger for both of them.

"She's in there, I *feel* it," said Joe. He shined his flashlight on the massive oak door of what seemed to be a Victorian mansion.

"The storekeeper was right—this is a crazy place," said Frank.

"When we were kids, we would have called an old heap like this a haunted house," said Joe. "Except it's not a ghost we're looking for." He reached for the doorknob. "Now we—" Suddenly Joe gasped. "Wha—?"

He and Frank were caught in blazing light that seemed to come from every direction. It blinded them, but they could hear a voice near them quite well.

"Freeze—or you will be the dead ones!"

Chapter

4

BLINKING, THE HARDY boys turned toward the sound of the voice. But the glare of a spotlight prevented them from seeing whoever was talking.

"You seem to be interested in entering the Lazarus Clinic," the voice said. It was remarkable in just one respect: There was nothing remarkable about it. It was without an accent of any kind. "Allow us to give you a guided tour. But first, raise your hands."

Two men dressed in black slacks, black sweatshirts, and black athletic shoes stepped forward. They carried military assault rifles poised and ready.

Frank and Joe raised their hands.

"I am glad to see you are being cooperative," said the voice. "Hugo and Fritz have nervous

25

trigger fingers. Now we must have a quick examination of your persons. Hugo, frisk them."

While Fritz trained his rifle on the Hardy boys, Hugo took their hunting knives from their sheaths, then gave them a swift but professionally thorough going-over, from their ankles to their shoulders.

"Good, you are clean," said the voice. "Take them inside."

Hugo swung open the door, and prodded by Fritz's assault rifle, the Hardy boys went inside.

From behind them the voice said, "Please do not turn around to look at me, unless you want a rifle barrel smashed into your face. Instead take a look around you. This building is unique. It was originally built ninety years ago by an eccentric millionaire, who later went bankrupt. It was converted into a mental clinic sixty years later by an even more eccentric psychologist, who went bankrupt in turn. It is now perfect for my organization to use. Not only did we buy it dirt cheap, but we are assured of privacy here. Our work demands a great deal of privacy."

"Pretty sloppy of you to leave your front gate unlocked then," said Frank.

He got the answer he half-expected.

"It was no accident that the gate was unlocked—for you," said the voice. "Rest assured, it is locked now."

"So we walked into a trap," said Frank. "And Iola was the bait."

"I was told you were an intelligent young man," the voice said.

"So it *was* Iola!" Joe exclaimed. "She *is* here! Tell me where she—" Forgetting himself, he wheeled around to question his captor.

He didn't get to finish his question—or see who was doing the talking.

All he saw was Fritz's rifle barrel slashing toward his face, while in the background, a figure darted out of sight behind a high-backed chair.

At the same time, the lightning reflexes that made Joe an ace athlete went into action. Before the rifle barrel could touch his face, he grabbed it and pulled it, letting Fritz set himself off balance by his own forward momentum. Then he viciously shoved it away, sending Fritz sprawling backward into Hugo's rifle.

"Run for it!" Joe shouted to Frank while he himself dashed through a nearby doorway and down a corridor. Behind him he heard shouts and running footsteps.

At the end of the corridor was a winding stairway. Joe went up it three steps at a time. On the second floor, he raced down another corridor, rounded a sharp turn, and found himself facing a closed door. The door was metal, in sharp contrast to the old wood of the house and the faded floral carpeting on the floor.

Joe heard the footsteps of his pursuers. He hesitated for just a moment before grabbing the door knob and giving it a turn.

The door opened easily. Joe stepped inside—and felt his knees go weak.

Stunned, he could only gasp, "Iola."

She was sitting in a chair facing him, looking exactly the way she did when Joe had last seen her—her face, her hair, even the clothes she was wearing.

But now there were electrodes fastened to both sides of her head.

Leather straps bound her wrists to the arms of the chair.

And her eyes stared blankly at Joe.

Iola wasn't alone. Four men were in the room. There were a distinguished-looking elderly man with a thick white crew cut and a livid scar across his pale forehead; a short, stout, middle-aged Oriental; a tall, thin youth in his twenties with a freckled face and horn-rimmed glasses; and a massively built man with a shaved skull. All wore white lab coats and the same startled expression as Joe barged in.

Joe, though, had eyes only for Iola.

"What are you doing to her?" he cried. He clenched his hands into fists and moved forward menacingly. "Take those electrodes off her head! Get those straps off her wrists!"

He didn't know what he was going to do if they refused—and he never got to find out.

Too late he heard a sound behind him.

Before he could turn, an arm snaked around his neck.

28

Then he felt a jabbing pain in his arm.

A needle— was all he managed to think before the room and Iola's face blurred as Joe slid down the chute to oblivion.

Oblivion, Joe decided, was like a sleep without dreams. There was no way of telling how long he was out. It might have been a minute or a day later that he opened his eyes and saw Frank's face looking down at him with concern.

"I was hoping you had gotten away," said Frank. "No luck, huh?"

"I was hoping you'd made it, too," said Joe, putting his hand to his forehead, which was aching from the aftereffect of whatever drug had knocked him out. Then he said, "Ouch!"

It wasn't his forehead that had pained him, though. It was his thumb. Only then did he notice that his thumb was wrapped in a thick bandage.

The next thing he noticed was that Frank's thumb was bandaged in the same way.

"Our thumbs," Joe said. "What happened to them?"

"I've been wondering the same thing ever since I came to after they drugged me," said Frank. "All I know is how much it hurts—too much to risk taking the bandage off."

"Cautious as usual, but I guess you're right," said Joe. "Anyway, we've got more important questions to answer. Like where are we, and how do we get out of here? I can't even tell what time of day it is. They took my watch away, along with my clothes. The sweatshirt and pants they put on me are two sizes too big. You're lucky. At least they left you with your clothes."

"They left me with my watch, too," said Frank, glancing at it. "It's ten P.M. We were knocked out for a whole day."

"Unless they fooled around with your watch to confuse us," said Joe. "In this room, there's no telling." His eyes traveled around the blank white walls of the windowless room. The only opening was a viewing window of unbreakable plastic in the metal door.

"Good thinking. We have to watch out for dirty tricks," said Frank, nodding. He looked around the room. "I can't see any way out of here. This must have been a high security cell for disturbed patients when this place was an asylum."

"We'll have to wait until they take us out of here, and then make a break for it," said Joe. "One of us has to make it. It isn't only for our sakes. Iola is here. I saw her, right before they caught up with me."

Frank leaned forward, his eyes gleaming with excitement. "That can only mean one thing. The Assassins are involved in this. They're the only ones who could have gotten their hands on Iola right before the car blew up."

"So you're finally convinced she's alive?" asked Joe.

"I can't deny the evidence," said Frank. "They must have yanked her away from the car

30

door a split second after she opened it and a split second before that device triggered the bomb."

"It's like I told you—I never actually saw Iola get in the car," Joe said eagerly. Then he paused. "But why would the Assassins want to kidnap her?"

"Who knows what plans they have?" asked Frank. "The only thing we can be sure of is that they're still operating all over the world. Exposing one of their plots and nailing a few of their killers was like chopping one tentacle off an octopus." He set his face in determination. "We have to get out of here. We have to alert the Network."

"But first we have to rescue Iola," said Joe, a touch of anger in his voice. It was just like Frank to think of the Network first and Iola second. Frank had his dogged sense of duty to the Network—even though that top secret government agency and its contact agent, the Gray Man, had made it clear that they'd rather do without the Hardys, if only the Hardys hadn't proved so valuable.

Joe was slightly mollified when Frank said reassuringly, "Of course we'll get Iola out of here. I'm not some kind of monster. But we have to make contact with the Network fast. We have to warn them about what's going on out here in the middle of nowhere."

"I guess you're right," said Joe reluctantly. "As long as Iola gets number-one priority."

"Of course I'm right," replied Frank, and

when he saw Joe's reaction to his smug tone, he again added, "And of course Iola comes first. But we can't just go with our emotions. We have to make plans to cover all possibilities. Like what if just one of us makes it out of here? What does he do then?"

"He has to waste a lot of time getting back to Bayport," said Joe. "That's the only place we can contact the Network from."

"We may not have that much time, if we don't want the Assassins to skip out of this crazy house," said Frank. "We have to figure out a way to contact the Network from here."

"Look, you were the one who insisted we take a total break from crime fighting," said Joe. *You* decided to leave our connection with the Network at home. Without that modem the Network gave us, we're totally cut off from them."

"It was dumb of me, I admit," said Frank. "But look, give me a rundown of how you'll make contact with them. Not that I don't trust you. But I want to make sure you'll do it exactly right if I'm not around. The Network won't tolerate the smallest error. They're really strict about total security."

Joe nodded. That made sense. Frank was the one who handled the computer hook-up that connected them to the Network's central Washington office. But Frank had taught him how it worked—

in case of emergencies like this one. Joe went over the procedure in his mind, opened his mouth, and then closed it.

"What's the matter? Your mind go blank?" Frank said. "Take a couple of minutes. See if you can remember it without my helping you."

"It's not that. I can remember it perfectly," said Joe. "But there's a good chance this place is bugged. That drug must have messed up your head. You're usually the one who thinks of things like that."

"Of course I did. I checked the place out," said Frank impatiently. "What do you think I am? An idiot? Let's not waste any more time. They might be coming for us at any minute. Just tell me the procedure so I can feel secure."

Joe looked at his brother more closely. Frank actually looked angry. The drug must still have been affecting him, or else his nerves were shot. Joe felt funny, being the cool, levelheaded one, instead of Frank. But if Frank wouldn't admit that there was no way to detect really sophisticated eavesdropping equipment, then Joe would have to be the one on guard.

"No dice," he said. "The Gray Man told us never to risk revealing the contact code. You know that as well as I do."

To Joe's amazement, Frank's eyes glowed with fury. Then he relaxed, and shrugged. "Okay, if that's the way you want it. Conversation over."

"Glad you've come to your—" Joe began.

Suddenly the door swung open. Fritz and Hugo were there, with their guns.

"Let's go," said Fritz.

Joe kept a sharp eye out for any chance to jump them, but they were too alert and professional. As they marched the Hardys down the corridor, they kept a perfect distance from Joe and Frank—too far away to be attacked, but not far enough away for the boys to escape.

"I wonder what's waiting for us," Joe said to Frank as they walked along.

"I have a strong hunch that they have a big surprise in store," replied Frank.

There was an odd mocking tone in Frank's voice, but Joe didn't have time to wonder about it.

"In there," said Hugo from behind them as they came to an empty door.

As they entered, Frank said in the same strange tone, "Hi, Joe."

"Hi, Frank," answered the young man waiting inside.

Joe looked into the face of that young man— and suddenly wondered if he had really come out of his drugged trance.

Or if maybe he was as crazy as the inmates at the Lazarus Clinic used to be.

The young man he was staring at was himself!

Chapter

5

FOR A SECOND, all Joe could see was his own face staring into his, as if he were looking into some kind of crazy mirror.

Then he saw more.

He saw that the double facing him was wearing Joe's own clothes—which must have been why Joe was wearing the gray sweatshirt and pants.

He saw that his brother Frank, the *real* Frank, was not standing beside him, but was strapped in a chair in the center of the room. Frank was wearing gray sweat clothes, too, while his own clothes were on whoever it was who was posing as Frank.

Joe didn't try to figure out what it all meant.

Instead he shot out a right cross aimed at the chin of the double facing him.

But the double reacted just as fast, blocking the

punch with his left arm and lashing out with a right hook.

Joe knew it was coming. He slipped it by pulling his head back sharply and dived at his opponent.

He missed and hit the floor with a jarring crash.

His double leapt on him but did not make contact. Joe rolled out of the way in the nick of time.

The two of them lay sprawled side by side on the floor. Then, at the same time, they jumped to their feet and stood facing off, panting and looking futilely for an opening in each other's defenses.

"That's enough," said a voice over a hidden speaker system. It was the voice of the unseen man who had directed the Hardy boys' capture. A voice without accent or inflection. A voice that could have been produced by a computer—or by somebody who wanted to give no clue to his identity.

"The experiment is over," the voice continued. "You two could keep fighting for an hour without either of you gaining an advantage. Joe Hardy number two is a success, a perfect replica of Joe Hardy number one, right down to the last reflex. Okay, men, take care of Joe One, before he exhausts himself trying to knock himself out."

Fritz and Hugo, who had been watching the fight with big grins, stepped forward and grabbed Joe by both arms. They shoved him into a chair next to Frank I. Frank II, grinning as well, used the straps on the chair arms and legs to tie Joe in.

Careful not to let his movements show, Joe flexed his muscles to test the straps. They held tight—no chance of a breakout. At the same time, he glanced around the room, and caught sight of the lenses of TV cameras in openings in all four walls, near the ceiling. Doubtless the cameras showed everything that was happening in the room to whoever was in command.

The voice came over the speaker again. Frank and Joe, listening closely, could detect a note of very human triumph in the mechanical tone. "Now that you are both comfortably settled in, allow me to introduce the team responsible for our successful effort. I'm sure that if your hands were free, you would want to applaud them. Gentlemen, you may come in."

The men who entered were the four Joe had seen in the room with Iola.

The voice first introduced the distinguished-looking elderly man with the crew cut.

"Meet Dr. Helmut von Heissen, one of the most brilliant plastic surgeons in the world. Unfortunately, the world does not know of the remarkable advances he has made in skin grafting techniques, since he was unable to publish the results of the splendid scientific experiments he performed while a young doctor at a Nazi camp.

"Our organization, however, fully appreciates his genius. We have given him a free hand and unlimited resources to pursue his efforts ever since we discovered him living in forced obscurity. The results you see before you—Frank Hardy Two and Joe Hardy Two—are your perfect doubles, all the way down to your thumbprints."

Involuntarily, Joe and Frank looked at their bandaged thumbs.

Seeing this, Dr. von Heissen smiled. "Do not worry, young men," he said, in English that was blurred only slightly by a German accent. "Your skin will grow back to normal in a couple of weeks, providing, of course, you live that long. On the other hand, if I may use that phrase, your prints will be fully operational on Joe Two and Frank Two in a day."

"You've got to be kidding," said Joe. "I've heard of mad scientists, but . . . " Joe shook his head.

The doctor's face hardened for a moment into a chillingly ruthless mask of hate. Then it relaxed into a superior smile again. "I assure you, my methods have been perfected. I only wish I could publish the results of my years of trial and error. But the world is not yet ready to accept the necessity of using human beings as guinea pigs to speed the pace of progress."

"You must be patient, Doctor," the voice on the speaker said soothingly. "The time will come when the Lazarus Clinic will be revered around the world as a shrine to your magnificent achievements."

Then the voice went on with its introductions.

"Of course, molding the body means nothing unless the mind is molded—and we have experts on that, as well," it said. "Meet our colleague, Colonel Chin Huan, formerly chief of the indoctrination section of the Red Army. It was he who engineered the remarkably successful brainwashing program used on American prisoners in the Korean War.

"If he had not chosen to side with the wrong political faction in the power struggle after the death of the Chinese leader Mao Zedong, he would doubtless still occupy a high position in his native land. But as it is, we have been able to let him utilize and further expand his expertise in controlling and programming the human mind. By this time, it may be safely said that a person's mind is putty in his skilled hands."

Chin bowed in the direction of the speaker. "Thank you for your praise, but it was impossible to achieve without the technical help of my comrade Peter Clark." He bowed again, in the direction of the tall, thin, freckle-faced young man with horn-rimmed glasses who stood behind him.

Peter Clark stepped forward to join Chin, and the speaker introduced him. "Mr. Clark was formerly employed by a pioneering electronics firm on the West Coast, until it was bought by a larger corporation and its pure research budget was slashed."

"They took away my laboratory, just when I

was getting into some really interesting stuff,'' Peter Clark complained in a high-pitched whining voice. He sounded very much like a five-year-old tattling on somebody who had stolen his toys.

"Fortunately, we are able to supply Peter with all the equipment he wants. In return he has supplied us with the most advanced techniques for computerizing and electronically implanting information into the human brain,'' the voice said.

"Really neat stuff," added Peter, with a pleased expression.

"Now you see what the staff of the Lazarus Clinic can do," said the voice.

"You mean you created two guys who look like us, and then programmed them to think like us?" asked Frank.

"Not created—recruited," replied the voice. "We found two young men with the right body types. Then, using our excellent file on your personal lives, we programmed that information into your doubles. We've also recorded your voices and videotaped your activities, and then programmed your speech patterns and motor abilities into Frank Two and Joe Two. But there is a difference between them and you. A big difference. They think what we want them to think. And do what we want them to do."

"You jokers have gone to a lot of trouble—but why?" asked Joe.

"That is for us to know and for you not to live

long enough to find out," answered the voice.

"But you must want us for something. Otherwise you wouldn't have bothered to let us live this long," said Frank.

"You're right. But since you obliged us by walking right into our hands, we have decided to use your presence as an opportunity to pump every bit of information out of what is left of your lives."

"Pump away—you're not getting a thing. Let Chin try his brainwashing stuff and see how far he gets," said Joe defiantly.

"Joe's right," Frank said, and added with calm logic, "You blew whatever chance you had of making use of us when you told us you're going to kill us anyway. Bad move."

The voice, however, did not sound disturbed by the Hardy boys' resistance.

In fact, it seemed to be enjoying its cat-and-mouse game.

"Let me assure you, Frank, there are far more painful things than death—things that can make death seem sweet. And let me inform you, Joe, that there are far swifter and more effective means than brainwashing to get what we want out of you."

The voice paused a moment to let its words sink in. Then it continued, "But I still haven't introduced the fourth member of our team. How rude of me. Let me do it now. Gentlemen, meet Ivan Boshevsky."

With that, the big bearlike man who had been standing behind the others stepped forward. His shaved skull gleamed in the light. His smile gleamed even brighter. His grinning lips parted to display a set of bizarre false teeth, a mingling of gold, silver, and stainless steel.

"Comrade Boshevsky was employed by the Soviet KGB during the regime of Joseph Stalin," the voice went on. "Unfortunately, after Stalin's death, certain of his methods of interrogating prisoners were called into question, and he was not only discharged, but forced to spend several years in the same labor camps where he used to send others.

"Needless to say, as soon as he was released, he sought other employment for his extraordinary skills, and we were only too happy to hire him. His work for us has more than justified our confidence. He has been invaluable in extracting the most jealously guarded bits of personal information from the most reluctant subjects. As I have indicated, he is a true master of making any human being in his hands beg for death."

Boshevsky stood in front of the Hardy boys. He gave them another hideous smile. Then he extended his hands in front of him. They were huge. He put them together and flexed them to limber them up. The sound of his knuckles cracking was like pistol shots.

In a voice eager with anticipation, he said, "I am ready to begin."

Chapter
6

FRANK LOOKED AT the torturer standing in front of him and steeled himself. He remembered what his karate master told him about handling pain. Concentrate on the pain when it comes, rather than try to ignore it. By focusing on the pain and judging exactly how intense it really is, your mind becomes occupied so that fear cannot enter it. It's fear that makes pain truly unbearable, and by eliminating fear, you can stand far more pain than is ordinarily believed possible. Frank hoped his karate master was right. He would soon find out.

Joe braced himself, too. He thought of the times that linesmen had piled up on him on the football field, or baseballs had bounced off his ribs when he was batting. Each time something like that had happened, he hadn't quit or even backed off. He'd just seen red and gone after the opposition even harder.

"Do your worst—and see how far you get," Joe said to Boshevsky and to the unseen person who was directing the horror show.

"If you think we'll cave in, you're crazy," Frank added.

The speaker sounded amused. "I wouldn't dream of hurting two fine young men like you. I realize how courageous and dedicated you are. Breaking you down would be a waste of Boshevsky's energy, not to mention a loss of valuable time. Especially when there is a much easier way to get the information we want." Then the voice barked a command. "Bring her in."

Joe looked toward the door, and his breath caught in his throat. He wanted to believe what he was seeing, yet didn't want to believe it. He felt joy—and pain.

"Iola," he whispered.

A guard had led her into the room, his hand gripping her upper arm as he half dragged her to stand beside Boshevsky. When the guard let her go, she made no move to escape. Instead she stood there with a dazed look on her face.

"Say hello to your boyfriend, Iola," said the speaker.

"Joe, what are you doing here?" Iola said. "What are they going to do to you?"

"Forget about me," said Joe. "What have they

done to you? Are you okay? I can't believe you're actually alive!"

But before Iola could answer, the speaker cut in. "Don't worry about what we've done to Iola, Joe. Worry about what we *will* do to her if you don't tell us what we want to know."

"You wouldn't—" Joe began.

"You don't think so?" the speaker said. "Men, convince Joe that we are serious."

Smiling, the Hardy doubles unstrapped Joe from his chair, grabbing his arms firmly when he tried to lash out in a desperate bid for freedom. He felt their grip and realized that they were as strong as he. That made sense, he thought. Doubles were doubles. Joe II had to be Joe's match, and Frank II had to be at least as well conditioned as Frank, who was in top shape.

Meanwhile, the guard shoved Iola into the chair in which Joe had been sitting. He strapped her in, and Boshevsky stepped forward. Once again he flexed his huge hands and cracked his knuckles. Then with the serious look of a craftsman at work, he reached out with one hand and grasped one of Iola's earlobes, giving it a sharp twist.

Iola screamed.

Joe felt his knees turn to water and his blood turn to ice.

Boshevsky was reaching for Iola's other earlobe when the speaker said, "That's enough for the moment. Joe has had a hint of what will

45

happen to Iola if he does not cooperate. Believe me, Joe, what you have just seen cannot compare with Boshevsky's ingenuity and enthusiasm in inflicting pain when he *really* goes to work. But perhaps you don't believe me. Perhaps you want to see more."

"No, no more," said Joe. He kept his eyes on Iola and avoided looking at Frank. He didn't want to see how Frank would react to surrender. Because Joe was about to give in. He would do anything rather than hear Iola scream like that again. "You win. I'll tell you what you—"

"Not so fast, Joe. Think for a second," said Frank, before Joe could continue. "How do you know this is the real Iola? Remember, these guys specialize in creating doubles."

"But her clothes, her voice," said Joe.

"The clothes would be easy," said Frank. "And clearly they can program voices. That would be no trick with a computer to analyze and reproduce voice prints. They could have tapped our phone to get our voices, and as for Iola, remember how she liked to send tapes instead of letters to her friends? They simply got their hands on one of those tapes."

Joe wavered. He looked first at Iola, then at Frank. Whom should he believe? His brother—or his own eyes and ears?

"Very good thinking, Frank," said the speaker. "We were told you had a fine deductive mind, and indeed you have. Unfortunately, even the best of minds can be wrong. And fortunately, it will be easy to prove it in this case. Joe, ask Iola anything you want, no matter how personal it is. If she is not able to tell you things that only you and she could know, you are free to believe that this lovely girl is not the girl you love. Do you have any objection to that, Frank?''

Frank was silent a moment. He bit his lip, thinking hard. Finally he reluctantly admitted, ''I guess not.''

''But I do,'' said Joe. ''The stuff I ask Iola isn't anything I want anybody else to hear—especially your goon squad here. I'm not going to have Iola perform in this human zoo.''

''You want to spare your true love from embarrassment as well as pain. How very touching,'' said the speaker mockingly. ''But I will agree to your request. You may speak with Iola alone in a room. But I warn you against trying to escape. It would be quick death for both of you.''

The speaker needn't have issued his warning. The room into which Joe and Iola were led made thoughts of escape impossible. Like the cell Joe had been in before, it was without windows, and the locked door was made of steel.

As soon as the door slammed shut, Joe and Iola turned to face each other. They would have liked to touch each other, too, but their hands were cuffed behind them.

''A man yanked me away from the car just before it exploded,'' Iola said desperately. ''Then

I was blindfolded, and I wound up here. I've been kept prisoner ever since. It seems like forever."

"It wasn't so long ago," said Joe, looking into Iola's eyes. "It seems like just yesterday we were together. Maybe that's why, deep down, I wasn't surprised you're alive. I mean, in my heart, I never *really* believed you were gone. It's so great to find out I was right. It's so great to find you. One thing's for sure. I'm never going to lose you again, not if I can help it."

He could see no answering spark of joy in Iola's eyes, though. It was clear why. Iola was still reliving her ordeal.

"I didn't know what they wanted to do with me," she said, her voice filled with remembered hurt. "Then, a couple of days ago, they told me you and Frank were camping nearby. They ordered me to lure you two into a trap. They threatened to let Boshevsky loose on me if I refused. But when I saw you in the woods, I couldn't do it. I turned and ran."

Iola shook her head at the memory. "I was praying you wouldn't be able to follow me here. But you did. I guess I knew you would. You and Frank make quite a team. But this time you were too good for your own good."

Iola was obviously in agony over their plight. Joe ached to take her into his arms to comfort her. It hurt him that he couldn't. And what he had to do next hurt him even more.

"Look, I don't want to ask you a bunch of

questions to prove who you are—but I have to," he said. "I mean, *I* know you're *you*. No other girl has ever made me feel the way I feel now. That kind of thing can't be faked. But I owe it to Frank to do what I said I would. You know Frank. He doesn't go by gut feelings. He needs facts, and he won't go along with me to save you from Boshevsky unless he has some."

"I understand," said Iola. "I wish now that I *weren't* me. Or that I had the nerve to say I wasn't or to tell you not to tell them anything even if they torture me. But I can't. I'm just too scared. You see, they made me watch Boshevsky work on somebody once. I know what he can do—and I can't face that happening to me."

She paused, then went on. "But I don't even know what they want to get out of you. Maybe if it's important enough, I'd be able to stand up to them."

"There's only one thing they could want to get out of Frank and me," said Joe, "and that's how to contact the Network."

"The Network?" repeated Iola, puzzled.

"It's a government agency that fights criminals like these," said Joe. "Frank and I hooked up with them after a group that calls themselves the Assassins blew up the car and kidnapped you. We helped the Network stop the Assassins before they pulled off a political murder—Senator Walker's, as a matter of fact. The man you were campaigning for when the car exploded.

"Anyway, the Network sort of let us halfway into their confidence. They gave us a way to contact one of their agents, a guy called the Gray Man, in emergencies. Frank's double tried to fool me into telling *how* we contact the Network, and I bet that *my* double tried to fool Frank the same way. They failed, so now they're trying this."

"But why would they want to contact the Network?" wondered Iola, her brows furrowing.

"Beats me, except that it has something to do with our doubles," said Joe. "They could do a lot of damage."

"So your secret is important," said Iola.

"It's important—but it isn't as important as you," said Joe, looking hard at the only girl he had ever truly, deeply loved. Then his mouth tightened. "If you *are* you."

"How can I prove it?" asked Iola with a helpless look in her eyes, as if she could see Boshevsky coming closer.

"Remember our first date?" said Joe suddenly.

"Of course," replied Iola. "I remember how I told you I thought you were rude for showing up late, and stuck-up for thinking I'd still go out with you."

"And remember how I apologized right then and there and won you over?" said Joe.

"You did not!" said Iola indignantly. "I *didn't* go out with you, and it wasn't until the next day when you said how dumb you had been and how sorry you were that we started getting to be

50

friends. But I don't see what—" Then she paused, and her puzzled face brightened. "I see now."

"That's right," said Joe, and went on with his questions. He asked about the first time they had kissed, about their first quarrel, of dream dates they had had and ones that had been absolute disasters. He asked about movies they had seen together, their favorite snacks, plans they had made. He ransacked his memory, and Iola remembered everything as well as he did.

After half an hour he said, "I'm convinced, you *are* you. The trouble is—" He paused, unable to finish his thought.

Iola did it for him. "I know. The trouble is, you don't know whether to be happy or sad about it. Because now you have to choose between me and this Network of yours."

Joe's jaw tightened. "There's no choice. You're the one I have to think about. The Network can take care of itself."

He went to the door and gave it a kick to signal the guards who were waiting outside. They opened the door and led Joe and Iola back to join the others.

"What did you decide?" the speaker asked.

"You win," Joe said, keeping his eyes fixed straight ahead. He didn't want to have to see the pained look on Frank's face. "What do you want me to tell you—as if I didn't know."

"Not very much. Merely your procedure for

contacting the Gray Man at the Network," the speaker said.

"Don't—" Frank started to say, only to receive a jarring slap of Boshevsky's hamlike hand across his mouth.

Instinctively Joe started to move to his brother's aid. The guards at his side grabbed his arms instantly.

"Don't lose your head, Joe," the speaker cautioned. "Remember what will happen to Iola if you do anything foolish."

"Right, right," said Joe, and forced himself to relax his tensed muscles.

"And now, the information," said the voice.

Joe spoke quickly, as if he wanted to get it all out before he had second thoughts. "We contact the Network through a special modem, which at the moment is hooked up to Frank's computer in his bedroom back home. The access code is Z-slash-two-three-four-one-one-slash-M-O-slash-six-six-three. The response identification code is T-I-slash-four-three-three-slash-seven-seven. Our identification code is H-A-slash-two-two-two-slash-eight-six."

"I am happy you have been so sensible," the voice said. "Since you are so sensible, I need hardly inform you that if you prove to be lying, Iola will pay the consequences."

"I know," said Joe, gritting his teeth.

"Good," said the speaker. "And now that you have kept your part of the bargain, I will keep mine. I promised you that you would feel no pain after you told us what we want to know, and you won't."

Joe felt the guards' hands tighten on his arms as Dr. von Heissen opened a black medical bag. He removed a hypodermic needle and a vial filled with amber liquid. Then he filled the needle and turned to Frank, who looked defiantly at him, determined not to show any fear.

Swiftly, expertly, the doctor gave Frank an injection. Frank's eyes widened for an instant, then closed as his head dropped and his body slumped.

"Frank," said Joe, barely able to choke out his brother's name.

So this is how we meet our end, Joe thought as the doctor reloaded the hypodermic and moved toward him.

"Gute Nacht," said the doctor as he stuck the needle in Joe's arm and pressed down the plunger.

That means "Good night" was Joe's last thought before he plunged into blackness darker than any night.

Chapter

7

THIS HAS TO be a dream, Joe thought.

It was like a dream—a dream that kept repeating itself.

Once again he was being shaken awake. Once again he was in the windowless cell. Once again he saw Frank's face above him.

But this time Frank was dressed as Joe was, in gray sweatpants and shirt.

And Frank's face wore the same slightly dazed expression that Joe's did.

"It is you, isn't it?" Joe asked.

"Sure is," replied Frank.

"And we're not dead?" said Joe.

"If we are, this isn't my idea of heaven, and I hope we didn't foul up enough to go the other way."

By now Joe was fully awake, his mind functioning.

"I wonder why they didn't kill us on the spot," he said. "I can't think of any more use they might have for us."

"They must have wanted to keep us alive but safely under control long enough to make sure that what you told them was true," said Frank.

He looked hard at Joe, and Joe had to avert his eyes as the awful events flooded back to him.

"Look, I'm sorry, but I had to do it," said Joe.

Frank tried to keep his expression rigid with disapproval, but he couldn't. His face softened. "I know you had to," he said. "I know how much Iola meant to you."

"You don't have to use the past tense," said Joe. "She's alive, remember."

"I'm still not totally convinced of—" said Frank, but when he saw Joe getting ready to argue, he dropped the subject. There were too many much more pressing matters to iron out. "I wonder how long we've been knocked out. I wonder if it's been long enough for our doubles to start doing their dirty work, whatever it is."

"I think we're about to find out," said Joe as he heard a clicking noise. "Somebody's unlocking the door."

The door opened slightly and the barrels of two hunting rifles poked inside.

"Hello again, my little deers," said a voice with a strong French-Canadian accent.

"You two back up against the far wall," said another French-Canadian voice.

The Hardy boys obeyed, and the two hunters who had nearly bagged them in the forest stepped into the cell—Henri, the bald and bearded one, and Jacques, the wiry one. Both still wore their hunting clothes.

"I guess I should be surprised to see you, but I'm not," said Frank. "Your story sounded a little fishy."

"It was a cover story that we didn't think we'd have to use," said Jacques, shrugging. "We thought we'd knock you off right then and there, and that would be that. But we had strict instructions to be sure to eliminate both of you at the same time, or it was no go. It was vital that no one find out that you had been wiped out."

"That makes sense," said Joe. "Otherwise those doubles of ours would be worthless. Nobody would believe they were us."

"And when you failed, you fell back on your second plan," added Frank. "You put us on Iola's trail."

"Which led us into this trap." Joe finished his brother's train of thought.

"They told us you two were smart," said Jacques, nodding.

"But not smart enough," said Henri. "Come on, let's get this over with."

"What are you going to do with us?" asked Joe.

"First, we are going to take a little walk in the garden," replied Jacques. "And after that—but we'll let you find out."

"Yes, we will make it a surprise," said Henri with a nasty smile.

Frank and Joe exchanged quick glances. They didn't need words to tell each other what they both clearly saw. Henri and Jacques were still angry at having been beaten in the forest. They were aching for revenge. Frank and Joe would have to be careful not to rub their itchy trigger fingers the wrong way.

The Hardys meekly followed orders as they were marched at gunpoint out of the cell, through the empty corridors of the clinic, and out a door into the abandoned garden. It was night, and the garden looked like a ghostly jungle under the full moon.

"You don't mind if we ask you some questions," said Frank as they walked. "I don't figure you intend to let us live long enough to tell anyone the answers."

"You figure right," replied Jacques with satisfaction. "This time you will not escape our bullets. Just do not try to make any false moves—or you will die even sooner than planned."

"Before that, I'd like to know who it is that's outsmarted us," said Frank in a resigned tone. "I bet it's the Assassins. They're your bosses, and they set this whole operation up to get revenge on us for fouling up one of their plots."

"You're right about us being members of the Assassins," said Jacques.

"But you're wrong about everything else," said Henri.

"I don't get it," said Joe. "How can you be working for the Assassins, yet *not* working for them?"

"The Lazarus Clinic borrowed us from the Assassins to do this job," said Jacques.

Joe still looked puzzled. "Borrowed you? You mean, like somebody borrows a lawnmower from a neighbor?"

"Exactly right," said Jacques. "The Lazarus Clinic wanted to cut you down, and the Assassins had the tools to do it. Us."

"Like you said, the Lazarus Clinic and the Assassins are neighbors, good neighbors," added Henri. "The clinic has helped us many times in the past—for large amounts of money, of course—and we were happy to return the favor, naturally, also for a fee. The clinic had no trouble paying it. They run a very profitable business.

"You would be amazed at how many people want to change their faces and their identities. You would be even more amazed to know who some of them are. And the size of the bonus we are getting for this job would absolutely astonish you.

"The clinic couldn't afford to haggle with us. This was too much of a rush job," said Henri.

"The Lazarus people had been shadowing you two for a long time, developing a foolproof plan to snatch you and rub you out in your hometown, with nobody being the wiser. But when they discovered you were coming so close to them, in the Maine woods, it was an opportunity to eliminate you that they could not pass up, even if it meant pushing their plans ahead of schedule and laying out big bucks for us."

"This was a golden chance to get rid of you without a trace," Jacques elaborated. "They could take care of you in the forest, and if that failed, they could lure you here. They are very careful people. They always have a back-up plan."

By then the hunters and the Hardys had reached a small clearing in the garden. The hunters told the boys to stop, raise their hands above their heads, and turn and face the hunters. In the moonlight the Hardy boys could see the rifles aimed straight at their hearts.

"So they needed two killers in a hurry, and they got you two from the Assassins," said Frank. He kept his voice calm as he repeated what the hunters had said. He didn't want it to sound as if he was desperately playing for time as he tried to figure a way out of this jam.

"That must be why Iola looked so confused when she saw me—they hadn't had time to complete her brainwashing," said Joe.

"What a smart young man you are," said

59

Jacques with thick sarcasm. "Yes, you are right. The girl was merely supposed to pretend to run away, so that you would go get your brother and come looking for her. Then when you both came back together, she was supposed to reappear and distract you enough to make sure you were sitting ducks for us."

"Instead, she really did run away, and you were alert enough to save yourselves," said Henri. "I tell you, that failure will not look good on our records when promotion time comes around."

"Still, it did not end badly," said Jacques. "I heard the Lazarus people saying that though your coming here to the clinic presented a slight element of added risk, it also had its good side. They were able to get a very useful piece of extra information from you by capturing you alive."

"I just hope they tell that to the Assassins—so our performance rating is not hurt," said Henri.

"I'm sure they will, after we make sure these two are never a danger again," said Jacques.

"But there's something I still don't understand. What interest does the Lazarus Clinic have in the Network?" said Joe. "Why should they be so eager to have our doubles make contact with them?"

"They did not tell us, and we did not ask," said Henri. "Our job isn't to ask questions, but to follow orders."

"Already we have wasted too much time talking," said Henri. He gave the Hardy boys a nasty smile. "Don't think we don't know that you two have been stalling for time. We have merely been playing a little game of cat and mouse with you. But now your time has run out."

"That's right," said Henri. "We were called off an important job in Quebec to come down here, and we must get back there quickly. We are scheduled to plant a bomb tomorrow."

"So we get this over with right now," said Jacques.

"Yes," said Henri. "I suggest you stop staring down the barrels of our guns and look down at the ground."

"We're not scared of facing you," said Joe. He was getting ready to make a leap at them. He might not stand a chance, but it beat just standing there and taking it.

"Don't get any smart ideas, Mr. Tough Guy," said Henri contemptuously. "I said look at the ground, and I meant it. To your right, next to that rose bush."

Lying there in the moonlight were two shovels.

"You brought those shovels here—and now you will get to use them," said Henri.

"That's right," said Jacques. "To dig your own graves."

"Pick up those shovels and start digging," ordered Henri, motioning with his rifle.

"We'll tell you when to stop," said Jacques.

"And when to die," added Henri.

Chapter

8

SWEAT SOAKED FRANK'S clothes as he dug. He and Joe had been deep in trouble before, but never three feet into their graves and getting deeper every minute.

Digging in the hole next to Frank, Joe was thinking the same thing. There had to be a way out. But all he could see was the dirt on his shovel. The dirt that soon would be shoveled back over him.

Then both Hardy boys heard the words they were dreading.

"Okay, boys, you've dug enough," said Jacques, motioning with his rifle for them to stop.

"I thought graves were supposed to be at least six feet deep," said Frank. "This one is barely up to my waist."

"Still stalling for time, I see," said Henri. "Well, we don't have any more time to waste. We have to cut out of here for Quebec quickly, the minute we're finished with you. And these holes are plenty deep enough."

Jacques nodded in agreement. "They will not have to hold you standing up. You most certainly will be lying down," he said.

"And nobody is going to come digging for you here," said Henri.

"So goodbye, Hardy boys," said Jacques, taking aim with his rifle.

"Let me dig just one more shovelful—to even out the bottom. I always like to do a job right, even if it's the last job I ever do," said Frank.

He didn't dare look at Joe. He could only hope that his brother picked up on his words.

Joe didn't dare look at Frank. He could only hope that he was hearing his brother right.

The Hardys looked at the two Assassins and felt a surge of relief when Jacques shrugged and nodded, and then Henri shrugged in accord.

Instantly the Hardys turned to the work at hand. They took firm holds on their shovels, turned, bent down, and dug deep into the black earth. Then they straightened up, with their shovels carrying full loads.

"Maybe you will be rewarded for your labors. Maybe they will plant roses over you so that your blood will nourish beautiful blossoms. You will become what in the sixties they used to call flower children," said Henri, chuckling at his own grisly joke.

"It's a pity this has to end so fast—playing cat and mouse with you has been fun," added Jacques, smiling, too.

"Yeah, a pity," said Frank. "I'd much rather be the one who has the last *laugh*."

Praying that Joe interpreted his raised voice as a cue, Frank flung his shovelful of dirt at Jacques, who was nearest to him.

His prayer was answered.

Joe's shovelful of dirt smacked Henri in the face at the same moment that Frank's hit Jacques.

Both Hardy boys followed up instantly, coming out of their holes with raised shovels. They smashed the shovels down on the Assassins' skulls with equal force—and with equal results.

Frank and Joe stood side by side, catching their breath and looking down at the two knocked-out killers at their feet.

"Good thinking," Joe said.

"Good thinking yourself," replied Frank.

"Now what?" asked Joe.

"Now we have to move fast," said Frank. "We have to catch up with our doubles, and that'll be hard. We can be sure that they've already checked out the information about the Network connection; otherwise the clinic wouldn't have decided that they were finished with us. I wonder how long we were knocked out."

Joe bent down and took a watch off Henri's limp wrist. As he had hoped, it was a calendar watch. "We've been out for a whole day," he said. "No wonder I'm starved." Then he grinned and added, "Of course, action like this always gives me an appetite. What I'd do for a burger and some fries right now. Or maybe a double-thick shake."

"You'll have to forget about food," said Frank. "We have to figure out what to do with these two bozos. Then we have to figure out how to escape."

Joe looked down at the two Assassins. "I've got an idea. They were talking about planting bombs. Instead, *we'll* plant them."

Frank nodded, "Right. But before we do, let's change clothes with Jacques and Henri. That way we might be able to get past any guards at the gate, which will save us the time of trying to tunnel under the fence. And we need to save all the time we can."

"Let's get to work on these holes," said Joe, grabbing his shovel again.

Twenty minutes later, Joe and Frank were in the Assassins' hunting clothes, and the Assassins were in the Hardy boys' sweatsuits. The two killers, bound and gagged, were also in dirt up to their necks. All they could do to express their feelings was make faint noises while their eyes bulged with fury.

" 'Bye now," said Joe, picking up one of their

rifles. "I hope this doesn't get you in trouble with your bosses. I'd hate to think of you spending the next few years cleaning dirty weapons and stuff like that."

"I hope the guards at the gate don't check us too closely," said Frank, picking up the other rifle. "I don't want to have to shoot my way out of any tight spots."

"Risk is the name of the game," said Joe cheerfully as he headed toward the gate.

For what seemed like the millionth time in their adventures, Frank had to shake his head at his brother's enthusiasm for taking on danger.

On the other hand, Frank had to admit to himself, life would be pretty dull without the kick of overcoming odds.

For instance, when they reached the gate and gave the guard stationed there a casual wave, and in turn were waved through by him, the surge of triumph and relief made the jittery sensation beforehand worthwhile.

Unfortunately, the feeling of triumph lasted only as long as it took them to reach their camping site.

By the time they arrived, after a half-hour of jogging along the overgrown forest trail in their heavy hunters' boots, they were breathing hard. By now the eastern sky was brightening with the first hint of dawn. Joe looked at where their tent and equipment had been, shook his head, and said, "They've cleaned out everything. They didn't leave a trace that we had ever been here."

"I guess we should have expected this," said Frank. "Let's check out the station wagon, though I've got a strong hunch what we'll find."

He was right. The spot where they had parked the station wagon was empty.

"What now?" asked Joe, still looking regretfully at where the station wagon had been. "Two months of hard work on the engine and a new paint job down the drain."

"We need wheels. We have to get back to Bayport fast," said Frank. "That's where our doubles must have gone—to access the Network on our computer. We have to try to catch up with them before they use it. And if we can't do that, we have to alert the Network before our doubles pull off whatever dirty trick they're planning."

Joe wiped his dripping forehead. Already the chill of the Maine night was wearing off as the sun cleared the horizon. It was shaping up to be a scorcher. "It feels like we're chasing our own shadows," he said, looking down the deserted blacktop road.

"Let's make it to town and see if we can rent a car there," said Frank. "Good thing Henri and Jacques had wallets stuffed with cash. I guess the Assassins don't believe in credit cards." Frank started jogging down the road. "Come on. It can't be more than a six-mile run."

Joe jogged beside him, matching him step for step, even though Frank kept pushing up the pace.

"Aren't you glad now I made you go on all those training runs with me last winter?" Frank asked his brother.

"Give me sprinting any time," panted Joe. "Or at least give me a pair of running shoes. I think somebody slipped lead into the soles of these boots."

Thirty-five minutes later, Joe spotted the general store where they had bought their shovels.

"There should be a crowd cheering us on—like at the end of the Boston Marathon," Joe said, gasping for air. "I could use some encouragement about now."

"Come on, slowpoke," said Frank, pushing up the pace still more. "Let's just hope that we find someone up this early."

Fortunately, the storekeeper kept country hours. He was sitting in a rocking chair inside his store, sipping coffee.

"Morning, young fellows," he said. "Back so soon?"

"Seems so," said Frank carefully. He gave his brother a warning glance not to say anything more, just in case the storekeeper wasn't talking about them, but about their doubles.

Joe nodded almost imperceptibly. He got the message.

"What happened, your car break down?" said

the storekeeper. "I told you that old heap couldn't be trusted when I filled it up with gas yesterday. You should have listened to me and taken my price for it and that car rental deal I offered you."

"Yeah, I have to admit, you were right," said Frank, thinking fast. "It gave up the ghost just ten miles from here. Some local farmer bought it for junk and put us up in his barn for the night. As soon as it got light, we hiked back here to take you up on that car rental."

The storekeeper looked the Hardy boys over and said, "A little ten-mile stroll, and you boys are sweating like that? Why, when I was your age, I could do that without breathing hard. Trouble with young folks today, you don't take care of yourselves."

"Right," said Joe, grinning. "I plan to turn over a new leaf. But at the moment, I'm not in shape to make it home by foot. About that car rental you mentioned . . .?"

"Come with me," said the storekeeper, getting out of his rocking chair.

He led them out of the general store and down the single main street of the tiny town. They reached a car rental agency, and the storekeeper unlocked its front door and ushered them inside. Then he put on a cap with lettering that read We Aim to Serve You Better for Less, and said, "Now, what model do you want?"

"The fastest you have," said Frank.

" 'Fraid that's going to cost you quite a bit," said the storekeeper. "Now, for a lot less, I can give you our special wreck-of-the-week bargain, guaranteed to get you there or your money back."

"We'll still take the fastest," said Frank.

The storekeeper's face was torn between the pleasure of making a nice profit and the pain of seeing money squandered. "Well, I reckon it's your money," he said with a shrug. "What'll it be, American Express, Visa, or MasterCard?"

"We're paying in cash," Frank said, pulling out a wallet bulging with hundred-dollar and fifty-dollar bills.

"Sorry about that," said the storekeeper. " 'Fraid I can't take cash. Against the franchise company's rules."

"Look, we'll pay extra," said Joe, pulling out a stuffed wallet from his pocket.

"Rules are rules," said the storekeeper, shaking his head. Then he looked at the bulging wallets in the Hardy boys' hands while his tongue worked itself thoughtfully around in his mouth. " 'Course, I happen to have a car I just might be willing to *sell* you . . ."

A half an hour later, the Hardy boys were rolling down the highway in a 1955 Buick Roadmaster, with tail fins that seemed to reach halfway to the sky.

"I hope this whale makes it to Bayport," said

Joe, at the wheel, pressing down as hard as he dared on the accelerator.

"Good thing we still have some cash left," Frank pointed out. "We're going to have to stop at every gas station on the way. This car must get about a hundred yards to the gallon."

It was early afternoon and ten refueling stops later, when the car engine wheezed to a stop. But by that time it had done its job. The Hardy boys were just four blocks from home.

They climbed out and pushed the car to the curb. Joe gave it a quick final look. "This baby is going to keep me busy for at least five months."

Just then a voice behind them said, "Man, Joe, don't you ever get enough?"

Frank and Joe turned and saw their pal Chet Morton. He was grinning at them, his mouth stained brown from the chocolate triple-dip ice cream cone in his hand.

"Just this morning you drove by in that ancient station wagon of yours," said Chet. "Now you've got another antique. What you plan to do, open up a museum?"

Frank and Joe exchanged quick glances.

"It was a bargain, I couldn't resist it," said Joe.

"Hey, you guys want to go to the pizza parlor with me?" asked Chet.

"Some other time," said Joe. "We've got a couple of things to do right now. Anyway, what about that diet you were going on?"

"Like you said, some other time," replied Chet. "I've got things to do, too, like try the new peppers-and-pepperoni special." Chet patted his ample stomach with anticipation, gave a goodbye wave of his hand, and headed for lunch.

"So our doubles arrived here this morning," said Frank. "Let's make it home fast."

But they had covered only a block when they were stopped again.

It was Frank's girlfriend, Callie Shaw.

"You're still in town?" Callie said. "When I saw you a couple of hours ago, you said you had to make some kind of trip, so we couldn't see each other tonight. And why on earth have you and Joe put on those hunting outfits?" There was a hurt look in her eyes. "I know you're involved in a lot of mysterious activities, but you've let me in on them before. What's the matter, don't you trust me anymore?"

"Look, Callie, I promise I'll explain everything as soon as I can," said Frank. "But not now, okay?"

"If that's the way you want it," Callie said, and turned on her heel and strode away.

"Sometimes I wonder what you see in her," said Joe. "Every time we get a case, she wants to horn in."

"You've got to be kidding," said Frank. "I wouldn't mind Callie's help right now, except I can't see how anybody but ourselves can help us out of this mess. I'm getting more and more jittery thinking about what we're going to find out at home."

"Too bad Dad's not around," said Joe. *"He* could help us."

But Fenton Hardy, the great detective who was the boys' father, was away with their mother, Laura Hardy, on a well-deserved Hawaiian vacation.

The only one at home was the Hardy boys' aunt Gertrude.

When she saw the boys come in, a worried look appeared on her face—a not uncommon occurrence. The smallest thing could set off alarm bells inside Aunt Gertrude—and her nephews provided unending sources of concern.

"What happened?" she asked. "Some kind of trouble? You raced out of here just a few hours ago without a word of explanation. And now you're back, wearing different clothes."

"No trouble," Frank assured her as he headed for the stairs to his room.

"Just a little change of plans," Joe added, and followed Frank up the stairs, three steps at a time.

Frank and Joe went straight to Frank's room.

"We've got to warn the Network," said Joe as Frank warmed up his computer. "It's a shame we had to ditch that scrambler radio they gave us." The Hardys had had to leave the radio behind while being pursued through the Adirondack Mountains by followers of the *Cult of Crime*.

"There's still the computer modem," Frank said, tapping the code numbers on his keyboard. But the screen went blank.

"What the—?" he burst out, opening up the computer's case. Then his face got bleak. "The modem is gone. Our twins must have used it and taken it with them."

"Then we have no way to get in touch with the Network," said Joe.

Frank nodded. "Not by electronic connection—and certainly not in person. If only they trusted us enough to let us know where their headquarters are . . ."

His voice trailed off as the computer's disk drives began whirring. "Hey, I didn't start any programs."

"Get back!" yelled Joe as the computer went up in a blinding flash.

Chapter

9

FRANK'S CHAIR TOPPLED as he threw himself backward. He hit the floor hard, then rolled to his feet.

Joe charged the rogue computer with Frank's bedspread in his hands, ready to smother any fire.

But Frank had already reached the wall and pulled the plug.

With a sizzle of electricity, the computer died down.

The Hardys stared at the smoldering wreck. "Looks like our twins didn't just steal the modem. They set up a nasty surprise if anybody tried to use it." He waved away a thin wisp of smoke. "Even if they didn't nail me, they certainly nailed my computer."

"Maybe the Network will give you a new one," suggested Joe.

Frank's face was grim. "Yeah. If we could get in touch with them." He slammed his fist against his palm in frustration. "If we just had a clue to where they are."

"It's the Gray Man's fault," said Joe angrily. "He should have told us where to find him, instead of keeping us at arm's length, like we were a couple of kids who'd spill the beans at the drop of a hat."

"The trouble is, he wasn't so wrong," said Frank. "After all, we did give the Lazarus goons the information they wanted."

"You mean *I* did," said Joe. "Okay, I admit it, so don't rub it in. But I'm not apologizing. I'd do it again, if it meant saving Iola. If that makes me a wimp, then I'm a wimp."

"Nobody's blaming anybody, and nobody's calling anybody a wimp," said Frank, putting his hand on his brother's shoulder. Frank sometimes got mad at Joe, but when it came to a pinch like this, he wasn't going to see Joe hurt. "Let's not worry about water under the bridge. We have to worry about what happens now."

"What happens now is we stare at your computer and it stares back at us and—" Joe shrugged and said, "We're beat."

But Frank wasn't about to throw in the towel. "When you're stumped by a problem, it means you have to look at it from another angle," he said. "We have to stop looking at this useless computer and look in other directions, starting with going through this room."

Joe shook his head. "What do you figure we'll find? Think our doubles left us a note telling us where they were going?"

Suddenly Frank said in an excited voice, "They just might have. Take a look at this."

He was examining a notepad on his desk.

Joe hurried over, took a look, and then said with disgust, "Come on, Frank, this is no time for kidding. That's nothing but blank paper."

"You know how I like to keep my desk neat— as opposed to yours," said Frank.

"That's putting it mildly," said Joe. Frank's desk was always a model of efficient organization, while Joe's looked like the aftermath of a tornado.

"This notepad is out of place, sitting here in the middle of the desk," said Frank. "One of our doubles must have used it."

"So what?" said Joe. "He took whatever he wrote with him."

"Let's see if he did," said Frank. Without explaining further, Frank emptied his pencil sharpener onto his desktop.

Joe leaned forward to watch. This had to be important, if Frank was soiling his precious work space.

Ignoring the shavings of wood, Frank took a pinch of graphite powder between his thumb and forefinger and sprinkled it on the notepad. Then he shook the notepad very gently, the way gold prospectors used to shake their pans when hunting for gold in streams, to separate grains of precious metal from the silt.

"Pay dirt!" Frank exclaimed, peering down at the paper.

The paper was no longer blank. The graphite dust had settled in indentations in the paper made when something had been written on the paper above it.

"Now if we can just read it," Frank said, squinting hard. What he saw was: 7864 9 St. "And then there's a couple of letters," he added.

Joe peered at the paper, his eyes straining to make out the faint black markings. "There's an *S* and an *E*."

"That's it. Seventy-eight sixty-four Ninth Street, Southeast. We've got it!" said Frank triumphantly.

"One little problem," said Joe. "We know the number, we know the street, but we don't know the city."

"But we can make a good guess," said Frank. "Washington, D.C., is the only city I know that has addresses like that. Its streets are designed to form concentric circles, and they're divided into different compass points."

"Anyway, it makes sense that the Network is located there," said Joe eagerly. "What are we waiting for? Let's go!"

"Let's do one thing first," said Frank, grabbing Joe's arm before he could dash out the door.

"What?" said Joe. "We're wasting time."

"Let's change clothes," said Frank. "We want to keep a low profile, and I kind of think that two guys in hunting clothes, carrying Remington hunting rifles, might attract a tiny bit of attention boarding the New York-Washington shuttle."

"Okay, but make it quick," said Joe, already on his way to his room to change.

Five minutes later he was back, wearing a pair of clean but very worn jeans and a white shirt with the sleeves rolled up.

"My good pair of spare jeans is missing," he said. "Guess who must have taken them."

"I found the same thing," said Frank, who had been forced to put on an old pair of corduroys rather than the pressed Levi's he saved for special occasions.

When they got downstairs, their aunt Gertrude confirmed their suspicions.

"I don't know what's come over you boys," she said. "Used to be that you wore the same clothes for months, until they had to be peeled off you. Today you come back in fishing clothes, go out in your best jeans, come back in hunting clothes, and now you've made another change."

"It must be a stage we're going through," said Joe.

"You could look it up in a psychology book,"

said Frank, and paused. "Look, Aunt Gertrude, could we ask a little favor?"

"What is it?" she said.

"Could we borrow your car for the day?" asked Frank. "We have to take a little trip, and ours broke down."

"I don't wonder," said Gertrude with a small sniff of triumph. "I always said you boys were foolish, spending all that time with those ancient cars that Joe digs up. No surprise that they keep breaking down. That's why I keep trading mine in every two years for a new model. I never have the least trouble."

Joe didn't mention that the main reason his aunt never had car trouble was that she never drove over thirty miles an hour and seldom drove more than ten miles at a stretch. He just said, "Well, maybe this has taught us a lesson."

"I certainly hope so," replied Gertrude.

"But, anyway, can we borrow your car?" asked Frank.

"Well . . ." Gertrude pretended to be thinking it over. But as the Hardys well knew, she had never denied her favorite nephews anything they asked. "If you promise to be careful, and to drive very, very slowly," she said.

"Definitely," said Joe as Gertrude opened up her handbag.

"Of course," said Frank as she handed him the car keys.

It was true what used-car salesmen claimed about cars that were owned by timid, elderly ladies. Aunt Gertrude's car was in great shape, at least at the start of the drive to New York. By the time Joe drove it into the parking lot at La Guardia Airport in New York, several years had been taken off its operating life.

But it had done its job. The Hardys were able to catch a shuttle flight to Washington just before the boarding ramp was wheeled away. And less than an hour later, they were hailing a cab at Washington National Airport.

As the cab drove up, Frank said, "Seventy-eight sixty-four Ninth Street, Southeast, please—and fast. It's an emergency."

The driver turned around to look at them. "You *sure* you want that address?"

Frank double-checked the address he had written down on a piece of paper. "That's it. Seventy-eight sixty-four Ninth Street, Southeast."

The driver shrugged. "Okay. It's your money," he said in a tone that clearly meant, "It's your funeral."

When they arrived at their destination, the Hardy boys saw why the cabbie had sounded so skeptical.

Seventy-eight sixty-four Ninth Street, Southeast, was in the heart of the Washington, D.C., slums, the part of the city that visitors to the capital seldom saw or wanted to see. The street was lined with decayed or abandoned buildings, and idle men lounged on street corners or in front of bars, looking as if they were aching to rip off any stranger. The air reeked with poverty and the violence that poverty bred.

"Want me to wait?" the cabbie asked. "You won't be able to hail a cab in this neighborhood. And you might not get one even if you phone."

"We'll take our chances," said Frank as he paid the man. "We might be awhile."

He waited until the cab drove off before he turned to Joe. "I wonder what our chances are. I've got a strong hunch we've fouled up. This doesn't exactly look like official Washington."

"Sure doesn't," said Joe, glancing at 7864 Ninth Street, Southeast. It was a five-story brick building that looked as if it had been built around the turn of the century and not been repaired since. Graffiti was scrawled on its walls, missing panes of glass had been replaced with dirty cardboard in many of its windows, and paint was peeling from its door. "Know what I'm thinking?"

"I'm afraid so," said Frank.

"We've got the wrong address," said Joe. "Which leaves us—"

"Nowhere." Frank finished his thought glumly. "But we might as well make sure."

He pressed the buzzer.

The front door was opened by a white-haired

man who was clearly the building super. He was wearing paint-splattered, grime-covered, tattered denim work clothes. But what was most noticeable was his size. He was at least six-feet-eight and close to three hundred pounds.

"What do you want?" he said in a hostile voice, looking meaningfully at the baseball bat he held in one hand.

"Uh, guess we have the wrong address," said Joe, stepping back.

"Yeah, sorry to have disturbed you," added Frank.

"Ain't got no use for strangers 'round here," the man muttered, and slammed the door.

"Well, that's that," said Joe. "We're back to square zero."

"Not quite," replied Frank.

"What do you mean?" asked Joe, with sudden hope. He knew the look in Frank's eyes. He could practically hear wheels spinning in Frank's brain. Frank had seen something.

"You notice that guy's work boots?" said Frank.

"No. I was too busy looking at his baseball bat," answered Joe. "Why? Something funny about a super wearing work boots?"

"Nothing funny about *ordinary* work boots," said Frank. "But those work boots had a high polish. The kind of polish the army likes its men to have. Or the secret service or the CIA or the

FBI or any other kind of organization. Some habits are hard to break, and shined shoes is one of them."

"So this guy could work for the Network, and this place could be a front," said Joe, nodding.

"It would be a perfect cover."

"It's easy enough to find out," added Joe. "We just have to buzz him again and tell who we are and ask to see the Gray Man."

"Think a second," said Frank. "How can we prove who we are? Our doubles have our IDs." He looked down at his bandaged thumb. "They even have the thumbprints that are on our IDs. That guy would never let us in."

"We could try to overpower him," said Joe. But he didn't sound enthusiastic about their chances of overcoming that man-mountain.

"There are some things even karate can't do," agreed Frank. He thought a moment. "But we could fake him out."

"What do you mean?" asked Joe.

"I'll show you." Frank picked up an empty bottle that was lying in the litter-filled gutter. Then he walked over to a boy who was standing nearby, looking at the Hardy boys curiously. The boy was about ten years old, wearing worn-out-at-the-knees jeans and a ripped T-shirt. His eyes lit up when Frank waved a ten-dollar bill in front of his face.

"Like to earn some easy money?" Frank asked him.

The boy looked hard at the money, then shook his head. "I ain't getting into anything illegal, mister. No way."

"Nothing illegal," said Frank. "And no danger—not if you can run fast."

"Fastest kid in my class," said the boy with pride. "What do you want to do? Put me in some kind of race?"

"That's right," said Frank. "A kind of race. See, the super in that building has been boasting to me how quick he is for his size, and how he doesn't have to lose weight. I want to show him he's wrong. So I'm setting up a test for him. You stand right here, and when he opens the door, make sure he sees you, and then you start running."

"He won't catch me, not in a million years," said the boy, pocketing the bill.

By now Joe had gotten the idea. "Let me have that bottle," he said to Frank. "I've got a stronger pitching arm than you."

"Just remember to duck out of sight fast," Frank said as Joe started his wind-up.

Joe's throw was perfect. The bottle smashed through a front window, and the Hardy boys were crouched behind a next-door stoop by the time the super appeared.

The boy was honest—he earned his pay. He waited for the super to spot him, then tore down the street.

The super went after him.

"That white hair has got to be fake," said Joe, watching him. "That guy moves like a pro half-back."

"We'd better move fast, too," said Frank, leading the way through the front door that the enraged guard had neglected to close.

"Wow," said Joe as he looked around him. "Who would have thought it?"

They weren't in a decaying tenement. They were in a modern office complex, with brightly lit corridors leading past rows of gleaming doors. In front of them on the wall was an office directory.

"Could this be it?" said Frank, his eyes scanning the list of names. " 'Edward Gray. Operations chief. Four twenty-two.' "

"Sounds worth checking out," Joe replied.

"Let's get in that elevator before somebody comes along and spots us," said Frank.

They entered the small elevator near them and rode to the fourth floor. There they followed the numbers on the doors until they reached 422.

"We won't bother to knock," said Frank. "It's a little late in the day to worry about being polite."

He swung open the door and entered, with Joe right behind him.

Joe breathed a sigh of relief. Their gamble had paid off.

The Gray Man was sitting there, behind the desk.

Even better, the Gray Man's eyes lit up when he saw them.

"Frank and Joe Hardy," he said. "What a surprise. Good to see you. What can I do for you?"

Joe grinned. Their troubles were over.

Except that Frank didn't seem to see it that way.

Joe's mouth dropped open as he saw Frank dash toward the Gray Man. Frank hurtled himself over the desk. He smashed into the Gray Man, toppling him out of his swivel chair. Then he sat on the Gray Man's chest and raised his fist menacingly over his deathly gray face.

Frank had gone crazy—or had he?

Suddenly Joe had a horrifying thought, and his blood turned to ice.

Was this really Frank, or was this—?

He didn't bother finishing his thought.

Instead he moved forward, his fists clenched, as he asked harshly, "Who are you anyway?"

Chapter

10

FRANK, STILL SITTING on the Gray Man's chest, looked up at Joe and grinned.

"Relax. I'm still me," he said. "And I haven't gone nuts."

"But—" Joe looked quizzically at the Gray Man, who was unsuccessfully struggling to get out from under Frank.

"I saw him reaching for his desk buzzer," said Frank. "He was going to sound the alarm and bring in guards to haul us away." He looked at the Gray Man, who had given up struggling. "Am I right?"

"You'll never get away with this," the Gray Man said, glaring defiantly at Frank.

"What's gotten into him?" Joe asked his brother.

"It's not what's gotten into him. It's *who's*

gotten *to* him," said Frank. "Our doubles must have arrived here already and convinced him they were us. So when we arrived, he thought we were imposters. Right, Mr. Gray?"

"Very clever," said the Gray Man. "But not clever enough to fool me."

"See what I mean, Joe?" said Frank. "That's why I didn't want him to call the guards. It would have taken too long to convince everybody that we're really us, especially if they tossed us in jail instead of hearing us out. I couldn't risk that. We have to stop our doubles before they do whatever they're out to do. What *are* they out to do, Mr. Gray? You must know. What did they come to see you for? We have to know their next move so we can stop it."

"I'm not talking," the Gray Man said, his jaw clenched with determination.

"Look, we're *us*," said Joe. "Can't you *tell?*"

"I can tell that those are convenient bandages—now we can't check the thumbprints in your files," said the Gray Man. "And I can tell that you're trying to bluff your way through this masquerade even though you've found out I'm on to your game."

Joe looked helplessly at Frank. "What can we do? The guy won't listen."

Frank's brows furrowed. Then they relaxed as he made his decision. But the grim look on his face made it clear that he wasn't happy with what he had decided to do.

"We can't waste time talking, Mr. Gray," he said. "We have to take more direct action."

Joe stared with shock as Frank stood up and hauled the Gray Man to his feet. In the same motion, he grabbed the Gray Man's arm and bent it behind him.

The Gray Man couldn't hide a grimace of pain as Frank gave his arm a slight twist.

"Frank!" Joe protested. He didn't mind doing what he had to do in a fight, but this was different. Torture wasn't his thing. He could take it and he had. Handing it out, though, was something else.

Frank ignored him. "Make up your mind—fast," Frank said to the Gray Man. His voice was rock hard.

"Look, Frank, we can't—" Joe began.

Frank cut him off sharply. "We do it this way. We don't have a choice."

"I don't see why," said Joe, giving his brother a searching look. Maybe he had been right the first time. This couldn't be Frank, who hated to see anyone or anything suffer.

"I've got a hunch that what our doubles are planning has to be stopped fast," Frank said impatiently. "If it means playing as rough as they do, that's the price we have to pay. We can't afford to lose time. It's a rotten trade-off, but it's the only option we have."

Frank's words didn't make Joe feel any less queasy, but they did tell Joe that this was his brother. He recognized their logic, the kind of logic that made Frank so different from him. Joe went by his feelings, and they told him that torturing a man for any reason was dead wrong. But Frank believed in using his head, and arguing with the way Frank summed up a situation was as hard as arguing that two plus two made five.

All Joe could say was, "Maybe you're right, but I can't watch this." And he turned his face away.

"Okay, Mr. Gray," Joe heard Frank say. "Tell us what those guys wanted, and spare yourself a lot of pain."

"Not on your life," the Gray Man shot back.

"Then don't say I didn't warn you," replied Frank.

His eyes still averted, Joe winced in anticipation of what he would hear next.

But what he heard was his brother's defeated voice, "Okay, Mr. Gray, you win. I can't do it. I thought I was tough enough, but I guess I'm not tough that way."

Letting out a deep breath of relief, Joe turned to see that Frank had let the Gray Man go and was standing with his shoulders slumped and a defeated look on his face.

Then Frank's face brightened as the Gray Man put his hand on Frank's shoulder and said, "You win, too, Frank. You've convinced me."

"We have?" said Frank, totally puzzled.

For once Joe could see something that his brother couldn't. "I get it, Mr. Gray. You figured that *real* imposters wouldn't mind torturing you to get the information they wanted. But *we* wouldn't. And you were right."

"I know I'm right," said the Gray Man, his usual decisive authority returning to his voice. "You boys have a lot of courage, but there are some things you can't bring yourselves to do— which is one of the reasons the Network can never completely rely on you. We, like our enemies, sometimes have to play dirty to win."

"And that's one of the reasons we'd just as soon not get hooked up too tightly with you," said Joe. "We'd rather fight crime our own way, with our own rules."

"But right now we're in this fight together," said Frank. "And we have to stop our doubles."

"First of all, tell me about those doubles," said Mr. Gray.

"It's a long story," replied Frank. "But to make it short, there's an organization that makes doubles for clients who need them for crime. They made doubles of us, even down to our fingertips, and they forced us to tell them how to contact you."

"But I made you swear never to—" the Gray Man began, then paused. "I suppose they used torture."

Frank shot Joe a quick glance, then said,

"Right. Torture. I'd rather not go into the details."

"Don't feel bad," said the Gray Man. "Everybody has his breaking point. But tell me more about this organization. What's it called? Where's it located?"

Frank was about to answer when Joe cut in quickly, "There's time for that later. Right now, we have to stop our doubles."

Frank nodded. "Joe's right. What are they up to? Why did they contact you?"

The Gray Man nodded, too. "We *do* have to stop them fast, and that'll be hard. They're clever, I have to hand it to them. They contacted me through the computer hook-up and told me they had to see me personally with information they couldn't risk anybody finding out about through electronic eavesdropping.

"After they got here and after they passed through all the security checks to be able to see me alone, they told me they'd gotten wind of a plot that concerned the life of the President himself. But when I asked them what it was, they said they couldn't tell me. And can you guess why?"

"I'll take a wild guess," replied Frank.

"Go ahead, Sherlock," said the Gray Man, with a smile. "That's what your brother calls you, if I remember correctly."

"Our doubles told you that they couldn't trust

you because there was an organization that made doubles of key figures and you might be one of them."

The Gray Man tried not to look surprised. "And how did you figure that out?"

"You didn't seem as surprised as you should have when we told you about the Lazarus group—like you'd heard it all before," answered Frank.

"So they're called Lazarus," said the Gray Man, thoughtfully.

"But what did they want with you?" Joe interrupted impatiently.

"Oh, right. Back to the subject at hand," said the Gray Man. "They said they could only speak to the head of the Network because they could be sure that this was one person whose identity this Lazarus group could not know. You see, I am the only one in the Network—and one of only a very few people in the highest level of government—who knows who the head is."

"And you revealed it to them?" said Frank.

For a second the Gray Man's air of assurance faded. He looked ashamed, apologetic. Then he pulled himself together. "I did. It was a snap decision and I made it. They claimed the President's life hung by a thread, and only the Network head could stop that thread from being snapped very, very soon. So I told them. Or rather, I told *you*. You see, though I have a lot of doubts about your maturity and efficiency, I have no doubts at all about your honesty."

"Thanks," said Joe.

"Anyway, there's a good chance we can stop them before they do any damage," said Frank. "You can contact your boss immediately."

"If only it were that simple," said the Gray Man. "But you see, one of the methods we've employed to keep our head's identity a total secret is not to have any mechanical lines of communication with the boss.

"I think, especially after seeing how hostile forces succeeded in finding out the link between you and me, that you can see our wisdom in doing that. Only I have contact with our head, in ways that no one shadowing me can suspect. That's just part of the security system that our head has personally devised, and it's proved to be the most effective cover a secret official has ever had— until now, anyway."

"Then you'll have to rush some of your men to cut off the doubles," said Frank.

"Letting our own agents in on the secret would break the system wide open," said the Gray Man. He went to his desk and pulled out a Browning automatic pistol and put it in a shoulder holster that he also took from the desk. He removed his jacket, fastened the holster, and put his jacket on again. "There's only one way to do it. We have to go ourselves."

"What a good idea. Let's all go together."

It was Frank's voice—but it came from the doorway.

Silently the door had been swung open, and Frank II stood there, with a Beretta pistol leveled. As he stepped into the room, Joe II followed, an identical pistol in his hand.

"Brother Frank is right," said Joe II. "I'm sure our twins here are simply dying to meet the Network head."

"Well, maybe we can arrange that," said Frank II, with the kind of sharklike grin that had never appeared on Frank Hardy's face. "First, they'll see the head. And then they'll die."

Chapter

11

"GOOD THING WE checked with home base before we proceeded with the plan," said Frank II as Joe II relieved the Gray Man of his pistol and pocketed it, then frisked the Hardys for weapons.

"Yeah," replied Joe II. "They told us that you two bright boys had escaped and might be coming after us. We were ordered to double back, wait outside this place in case you arrived, and then put you and Mr. Gray out of action."

"Contingency Plan A," added Frank II. "The boss covers all bases when he sets up a job."

"Thanks to you boys, we had to junk our original mission," said Joe II.

"A real shame." Frank II shook his head. "It was a doozy of a scheme. The boss's best ever."

"But at least we'll accomplish something,"

said Joe II. "We'll get rid of the head of the Network, Mr. Gray, and of course you two."

"You'll never get away with this," said the Gray Man. "You'll never even get out of this building."

Frank II smiled. "I don't think we'll have any trouble."

"The boss told us what to do," said Joe II. "We just walk out."

"With you and the Hardy boys," added Frank II. He was wearing Frank's favorite seersucker jacket. He put his pistol hand in the pocket but kept the gun pointed at the Gray Man.

Joe II put his pistol hand in the pocket of the windbreaker he had taken from Joe's closet. He, too, kept his weapon on the Hardy boys.

"Now let's walk out of here together, nice and slow," said Frank II.

"And what will the guard think when he sees two pairs of Hardy boys?" asked the Gray Man.

"The boss thought of that—like he thinks of everything," replied Joe II. "He said this was one place where nobody would even blink."

"Yeah, he said Network people would be used to seeing weird stuff," said Frank II. "They'd figure using doubles was just a new trick of the trade."

Their boss was right. The guard didn't blink an eye when he saw them. In fact, he opened the door for them to go out.

The doubles shepherded Mr. Gray and the

Hardy boys down the street and around a corner. There a large black Mercedes waited for them.

"You guys do things in style," remarked Joe.

"Money is something we don't have to worry about," Joe II replied.

"Yeah. Whoever said that crime doesn't pay never heard about us," said Frank II. He pulled his gun out of his pocket and motioned for the Hardys to sit in the backseat. Then the doubles got in front, with Mr. Gray squeezed between them.

"Don't you two get any funny ideas back there," said Joe II. "My gun is going to be pressed against Mr. Gray here the whole ride. One false move from either of you, and he gets it."

"Just sit back and enjoy the scenery." Frank II pressed the starter and the engine purred to life. "It's your last trip, so you might as well make the most of it."

Frank and Joe exchanged looks, each hoping to see in the other's eyes a gleam of inspiration, a bright idea for getting out of the jam. But there was nothing.

They turned away from each other and looked out the car window as they drove out of the city slum and over a bridge spanning the Potomac River. Soon they were traveling through a countryside that seemed a world away from the mixture of grandeur and grime that was the nation's capital. They saw green fields divided by low stone walls, untouched stands of forest, rippling brooks, and large mansions set far off the highway.

"Pretty cool, huh?" remarked Joe II. "Fairfax County, Virginia. This is where the rich folk live. You know, the fox-hunting set."

"Except we're doing a different kind of hunting," said Frank II. "Head hunting."

"You guys are real jokers," Joe replied sarcastically.

"Yeah, a riot," added Frank.

"Glad you think so," said Joe II. " 'Cause then you can die laughing."

"And you won't have long to wait for the punchline," said Frank II as he turned the Mercedes off the main highway, passing a sign that read Allingham Manor, and onto a narrow blacktop road that cut through a stand of forest.

"Wow!" exclaimed Joe as the road emerged from the forest and he saw an immense, beautifully tended lawn gleaming emerald in the late afternoon sunlight. In the distance was a large, white mansion with Grecian columns.

Joe peered at the house as they approached it. "It looks like something George Washington could have lived in at Mount Vernon."

"Or Jefferson, at Monticello," added Frank.

"But definitely not the kind of place that the Network head would live in," said Joe II. "Pretty shrewd."

"But not shrewd enough." Frank II stopped the car on the white-pebbled circular driveway in front of the mansion.

"This is where we get out," said Joe II. With his gun pressed against the Gray Man, he eased out of the car and his "brother" did the same. They motioned for the Hardys to follow. When they did, the doubles put their pistols back in their jacket pockets, but kept them at the ready.

"And how do you figure on getting past the guards here?" asked Frank. "What kind of brilliant plan did your leader come up with?"

"That's the beautiful part," replied Joe II, smiling at a private joke.

"No plan needed," said Frank II with the same kind of grin. "You tell them, Mr. Gray. If I did, it would crack me up."

The Gray Man, a pained expression on his face, cleared his throat uncomfortably and said, "Unfortunately, there are no guards here."

"No guards?" repeated Joe, baffled.

"But you must have some kind of security," said Frank, and then paused, not wanting to say more. He didn't want to tip the Gray Man's hand. Maybe the Gray Man had been on to their doubles from the very first and was laying a trap for them.

"No, he's not fooling you—or us," said Frank II, as if he had been reading Frank's mind.

"Come on, Mr. Gray, explain the setup here to

these two bright boys, just like you explained it to us when you thought we were them," said Joe II, enjoying the Gray Man's discomfort.

"It's the chief's idea," said the Gray Man defensively. "Actually, it's quite brilliant. The idea is that the best security system is no security system at all. Even the most cleverly disguised guards can be spotted through their own lapses or through leaks in the organization that hires and trains them. So the chief does without all the usual protection and lives completely in the open, which is the most ingenious cover ever devised."

"Talk about being too smart for your own good," said Frank II. "Your boss takes the cake."

"Our boss told us this job would be no sweat," added Joe II, "but even he didn't suspect how easy it would be."

Frank II rang the front doorbell, and a formally dressed butler answered. When he saw the Gray Man, he bowed his head slightly in recognition.

"Come for a visit, sir?" the butler asked.

The Gray Man glanced at the pistol bulging in Joe II's jacket, then said, "That's right, Harvey."

The butler ushered them inside and said, "Please wait in the drawing room while I announce your arrival."

The butler left them and started up a winding stairway while the Gray Man led the others into a large, elegant drawing room. It was painted a delicate robin's-egg blue and was furnished in the style of the eighteenth century, complete with a gleaming harpsichord.

"Your boss has refined taste for somebody in such a tough racket," Frank II commented, looking at the paintings on the wall.

"A lot of things about the chief would surprise you," said the Gray Man.

The Gray Man was putting it mildly.

At that moment, the Network head entered the room, after dismissing the butler at the doorway.

The doubles' jaws dropped open. The Hardy boys were just as startled.

"What brings you here, Gray? Our next meet isn't scheduled until the fox hunt on Saturday," she said.

There was a sharp glint of suspicion in the eyes of the slender, white-haired woman as she looked at the Gray Man and then at the Hardy boys and their doubles.

"What is this? Some kind of masquerade?" she asked. Her hand moved toward the expensive purse she was carrying. It was slung from the shoulder of an exquisitely tailored summer tweed jacket that made her look as if she had stepped out of a fashion ad for gracious country living.

"Freeze, baby," said Frank II as he whipped his gun out of his pocket before she could open her bag.

"Toss that bag here—closed," ordered Joe II, pulling out his gun, too.

The woman's face did not change expression,

as if facing a pair of guns was the most natural thing in the world. With a slight shrug, she tossed the bag to Frank II.

He opened it immediately. "A Browning automatic," he said. "That's a pretty big piece for a nice little old lady to be carrying."

"Cut the jokes," she said. "What's going on here, Gray? Did you foul up?"

"Let me explain how it—" the Gray Man began.

"Yeah, he fouled up," Frank II interrupted.

"Don't worry, though," said Joe II. "He's going to pay for it."

"Unfortunately, lady, so are you," said Frank.

"This must be some kind of mistake," the woman replied. "My name is Laura Van Appels and I have no idea what you want with me. If it's loot you're after, please just take what you want and go. I'm sure Mr. Gray has somehow divulged that you can ransack this place without fear—I detest guards and burglar alarms. They're so vulgar. That's why I carry that dreadful gun in my purse, though I hardly know how to use it."

"Nice try, Laura baby, but no cigar," said Frank II.

"But don't feel bad, you had a great cover," added Joe II.

"No way would we have cracked it without help from your friends here," said Frank II.

"But all good things have to end." Then, in a curt voice, Joe II commanded, "All of you sit down against the wall, cross-legged, three feet from one another, with your hands tucked under you."

Laura Van Appels and the Gray Man obeyed immediately, but Frank and Joe hung back. Each was desperately looking for a way to get the guns out of their doubles' hands.

But the guns stayed in those hands, pointed dead at the Hardy boys.

"Come on, you two, move it," Joe II ordered, and Frank and Joe joined the others sitting cross-legged against the wall.

They watched helplessly as Frank II removed a roll of thin wire from his pocket, along with a wire cutter, while Joe II kept the captives covered.

Swiftly and expertly Frank II bound the hands and feet of the Gray Man and his boss.

"Don't move, and the wire won't cut into your skin," he advised them as he stood up and inspected his handiwork with satisfaction.

Then he turned to the Hardy boys. "Now for you two," he said.

Frank and Joe had the same thought. Maybe when Frank II tried to bind them up, they'd have a chance to—

But their plan died before it could be born.

"Get to your feet and stand in the middle of the room," Frank II ordered.

After the Hardys had reluctantly obeyed, Frank II said, "Now to finish setting the scene." He pulled the bell cord to summon the butler.

The butler was right on the job. Two minutes later he came through the door, and Frank II, pressed against the wall next to the door, brought his pistol butt down on the butler's head.

The butler dropped in a heap on the carpet.

"I bet you wonder what we're doing," Joe II said, grinning at the Hardy boys.

"I can guess," replied Frank, who had been following the sequence of events keenly, putting it together like a jigsaw puzzle in his mind.

"Okay, tell us, if you're so smart," said Frank II.

"You shoot the butler and the two tied up over there with your Berettas. Then you shoot us with the Browning. Next you put the Berettas in our hands, and the Browning in the butler's hand so when the police arrive, it looks as if we killed the Gray Man and Laura, then were surprised by the butler, whom we had knocked out, but who came to before we thought he would. He shot us, but not before we shot him. I bet you even have an extra gun in your pocket to plant on the butler, since you couldn't have counted on Laura packing one."

"*Very* good. It's like you can read my mind," said Frank II, pulling out the spare gun from his pocket. "But I guess I shouldn't be surprised. After all, your mind *is* my mind—of course, they left out your goody-goody conscience." He smiled. "Let me tell you, it's a real pleasure being programmed to be as smart as you. The boss told me that I would have the brains to come up with something good on the spot, and now I know where those brains come from."

"Yeah," Joe II said to Frank. "It's a real pity you aren't a little smarter."

Frank II agreed. "It's a crying shame. But I've thought and thought, and even with all your brains, I can't figure out how you can get out of this alive."

Chapter

12

SOMETIMES BRAINS AREN'T enough to save you.

Sometimes you need luck. Pure, dumb luck.

That fact was brought home to Frank Hardy at the very moment when he had given up trying to use his brains.

He heard a groan from the butler, who was lying on the carpet, and saw the man start to sit up.

Joe heard and saw the same thing.

So did Frank II and Joe II.

None of them had time to think about what they were doing.

Both Frank II and Joe II instinctively turned to handle the butler.

And in that split second, Frank and Joe made their move.

Frank karate-chopped Frank II's gun hand, sending the Beretta flying.

Joe slammed into Joe II, knocking him off balance. Before Joe II could recover, Joe had twisted his arm behind him and forced him to drop his gun.

So far, so good.

But then the Hardy boys ran into trouble.

Double trouble.

Frank's double easily parried what should have been a knock-out chop and stood facing Frank, looking for an opening to deliver a blow of his own.

Joe's double freed himself from Joe's hold by suddenly relaxing his muscles, then yanking his arm loose in the split second when Joe was readjusting his grip, a ploy that Joe himself had often used in the past.

Facing Joe II, Joe remembered the slugfest he had had with his double back at the clinic. Neither of them had been able to come out on top before the fight had been broken up.

Joe looked Joe II in the eyes and saw the reflection of his own face in those eyes that could have been his own. It was crazy, he thought, like looking down some kind of fun house hall of mirrors, seeing endless reflections of himself, until he hardly knew who he was and where he was. He felt dizzy.

Joe had to get a hold of himself. He clenched

his fists, cocked his right hand, and threw it. But Joe II easily blocked the punch, and then followed with a lightning right cross of his own.

Joe jerked back his head just in time and felt the fist whiz by an inch from his chin. Instantly he countered with a vicious left hook. It hit empty air as Joe II jerked his head back.

Again they faced each other, and Joe II grinned. "Just like before. You can't lay a hand on me," he said. "I've got all your moves and all your speed. But maybe they've programmed a few tricks into me that you don't have. This is going to be a real interesting fight."

Meanwhile, Frank and Frank II were circling each other, feinting, trying to find or force a chink in the other's defenses. Finally Frank lashed out with his foot in a kick that his teacher would have applauded, only to be caught easily by Frank II and thrown to the ground.

But when Frank II tried to follow up his advantage by jumping on top of Frank, Frank rolled out of the way and leapt to his feet. Frank II instantly followed, and once again they were circling each other warily, both breathing hard.

"Logically, neither of us can win," said Frank II. "Unless, of course, the clinic gave us a winning edge over you."

"We'll have to find that out," said Frank, refusing to stop hunting for some way to get at his double, while carefully keeping up his guard.

But it was Frank II who made the next move—a dirty move.

He leapt back, grabbing a sherry decanter from one of the elegant tables. With one motion, he whipped out the stopper and threw the wine into Frank's and Joe's eyes, blinding them.

But even through the pain, Frank's first thought was for his brother. He turned his head to see Joe II cocking his right hand for a savage punch.

At the same moment and in the same pain, Joe instinctively checked out his brother's safety. He saw Frank II readying a killer chop that could snap Frank's neck like a brittle twig.

Frank forgot his pain as he leapt to his brother's defense, catching Joe II's right arm with a chop that paralyzed it, then following it with a chop that sent Joe II to the floor. Joe II twitched once, then lay there unconscious.

Meanwhile Joe had jumped Frank II, who saw his fist coming a fraction too late. A moment later, Frank II was out on the floor, with Joe standing over him, blowing on his bruised knuckles.

"They forgot to program one thing into my double," Frank said. "They didn't know how often I have to get you out of trouble."

"*You?* Get *me* out of trouble?" cried Joe indignantly. "If I hadn't come to your rescue all those times with my right hand, you'd be a long-gone karate kid by now."

"Anyway," said Frank, "the clinic apparently doesn't know what it means to be brothers. Our doubles had a blind side."

"And we blind-sided them. No sweat," replied Joe, sounding a lot more cocky than he felt. He had been as close as he ever wanted to come to feeling he couldn't win a one-on-one fight.

Laura Van Appel's voice cut into their conversation. "Save the self-congratulations for later, boys. Get us out of these wires. We have work to do. We have to clean out the rats' nest that spawned those two." The authority in her tone told the Hardys why she was head of the Network. She was definitely a person who expected her commands to be obeyed instantly.

"Right," said Frank, moving toward her and the Gray Man.

"Hold it, Frank," said Joe sharply. "I have to talk to you about something."

"Talk to me? About what?" replied Frank, puzzled.

"And in private," Joe added.

"Hey, what are you waiting for?" said Laura Van Appels, with a touch of annoyance.

"Come on, kids, let's not fool around." The Gray Man suddenly looked uneasy.

"Let's talk in the next room," said Joe. "But first, let's tie up our doubles and the butler, too. We don't want them coming to before we get back in here."

"I can see tying up the bad guys, but why the butler?" asked Frank.

"I'll explain—in private," was all Joe would say. The serious look in his eyes made it clear that he didn't want to explain further.

"I hope you have a good reason for this," said Frank, as he and Joe set about tying up the butler, who was half-conscious now, and the doubles, who were still out like lights.

"Trust me," said Joe.

"Do I have a choice?" asked Frank.

By then both the Gray Man and his chief were fuming.

"Free us this minute!" Laura Van Appels commanded in a voice that was close to a bellow of rage.

"Wait until I get my hands on you crazy kids!" exclaimed the Gray Man.

Joe cut their voices off as he led Frank into the hallway and shut the door.

"What's with you?" asked Frank. "This better be important."

"It *is* important," Joe said fervently. "Nothing could be more important. Don't you see, we can't let them know all about the Lazarus Clinic—not when Iola is still prisoner there. I don't want to think what could happen to her if the Network launched an attack on the clinic."

"But I'm sure the Network would take all possible precautions," said Frank.

"Are you kidding?" Joe cut him off. "The Network's not going to do anything that would hurt their chances of wiping out Lazarus. You know as well as I do how the Network looks at things. If Iola got hurt during their attack, they'd just call it an unavoidable trade-off."

Frank wanted to disagree—but he couldn't. That *was* the way the Network operated. It might be good for national security, but it left a bad taste in his mouth just as it did in Joe's. There were some things the Hardy boys couldn't swallow, and sacrificing individual human beings in the name of the greater good was one of them.

Still, he couldn't help protesting, "We could get in a lot of trouble if we didn't tell the Network everything they want to know."

"And since when has trouble started scaring you?" asked Joe. He grinned at his brother. "Besides, I would have thought figuring out a plan to get Iola out of the clinic before the Network went in after Lazarus would appeal to you. I mean, you're always saying how dull life is without challenge and adventure."

Frank grinned back. His brother knew him too well. Iola might be Joe's weakness. Figuring out how to beat dangerous odds was his. Already his mind was racing, like a computer whirring into operation.

"I might just be able to come up with a scheme . . ." he said thoughtfully, and slapped the palm of Joe's hand.

"Ouch," said Frank, playfully flexing his hand to make sure it was still intact.

"That's nothing compared to what your jaw would have felt like if you hadn't agreed," said Joe. "Nobody, including you, is going to stop me from saving Iola."

"No way could you get past my guard," said Frank. "It's lucky you didn't have to try. And even luckier that you have me to figure out how we pull this off. On your own, you'd probably have broken into the clinic like you hit a football line—and gotten thrown for a dead loss."

"I won't argue, Coach," said Joe, "just so long as you get busy at the blackboard and draw up a touchdown play."

Frank had formed his plan by the time he and Joe returned to the drawing room ten minutes later.

Laura Van Appels and the Gray Man were seething.

"Cool it," said Joe, ignoring their demands to be freed. "I'm sure somebody will come along to untie you in a couple of hours or so. You must have a flock of servants in a monster mansion like this."

"We were thinking of calling the cops after we left here and having them come," said Frank. "But we figured you wouldn't want your cover blown. This way, you'll only have to explain things to the servants, and I'm sure you can come up with a good story."

"At least you're sane enough to have thought of that," said Laura Van Appels, her voice dripping with sarcasm.

"You'd better believe we know what we're doing," replied Frank. "And you'd better listen hard to what we want you to do. As soon as you're able, assemble a mobile strike force that can move fast by helicopter. Then have someone in this house ready to answer the phone and relay our message to the strike force when we contact you, since Network headquarters can't be reached by phone. We'll get the number on the phone in this room. Understood?"

"You'll never get away with this!" the Gray Man roared after them as they headed out the door.

Joe paused in the doorway and said over his shoulder, "You'd better pray that we do."

Chapter
13

THE HARDYS HAD recovered their credit cards and wallets from their doubles, which made travel much easier. They took a plane from Washington to Boston. There they rented a car for an after-midnight drive to Maine. The sun was just clearing the horizon when they pulled up in front of the general store where they had bought their shovels, and then the Buick Roadmaster.

As before, the proprietor was up early, sitting in his rocking chair, sipping coffee.

As soon as he saw them, he said, "Now, if it's about that Buick, I didn't make any guarantees. You bought it fair and square, and the store policy is clearly posted." He pointed to a tiny sign half-hidden behind a stack of bags of fertilizer. It read No Refunds.

"No problem about the car. It's a beauty," Joe reassured him.

"We're here to buy something else," Frank said.

"Well, what can I do for you boys?" the store-keeper asked, instantly getting to his feet. "I can offer you a great buy on a Pontiac convertible in the garage. Nineteen forty-nine model. Let me tell you, they don't make cars like that anymore. Needs a tiny little bit of work, of course. That's why I'll give you a real good price on it."

"Maybe another time," said Joe.

"Right now what we need is two shovels," added Frank.

The storekeeper gave them a look usually reserved for small children.

"Two *more* shovels?" he asked.

"Right," replied Frank. "We liked the first ones so much we want to give some to our friends as gifts."

"Good idea," said the storekeeper warily, keeping an uneasy distance from them. "I'm afraid, though, the price has gone up a little bit."

"But we just bought those shovels a few days ago," protested Frank.

"Got the manufacturer's notice in the mail yesterday," said the storekeeper.

"Okay, no argument," said Joe, pulling out his wallet. "And give us some rope, too. Real strong rope. I hope inflation hasn't hit that, too."

"Matter of fact, I just got the word about that, too, in the same mail delivery," said the store-keeper.

Carrying their purchases, Frank and Joe headed back to the car.

"It's not only open season on deer around here, it's open season on tourists," said Frank.

"Forget about those few bucks, tightwad," replied Joe, "because it's open season on the Lazarus Clinic for us."

Frank saw the eager, reckless look in Joe's eyes and cautioned, "Remember, don't go off half-cocked when we get there. Stick to the plan. Both plans, if necessary."

"You and your plans," said Joe. "One plan isn't enough. You have to come up with two. Myself, I'd rather play it by ear."

"We'll play it to win," Frank answered. "Developing plans and back-up plans is a good idea. So we go with plan A, and if we get into trouble, we switch to plan B. That gives us two chances instead of one to get Iola out of there."

Joe shrugged. "If that's what it takes, then that's what we'll do."

After parking their car and following the overgrown forest trail to within a few hundred yards of the fence gate, Frank and Joe put plan A into operation.

They left the trail before they came in sight of any guard who might be posted at the gate, worked their way through the forest until they reached a remote section of the high wire fence, and then started digging.

"I wish we could have waited until night," Frank said as he and Joe fell into the rhythm of their work. First Joe would dig a shovelful of dirt. Then, while he was tossing it over his shoulder, Frank would take one. The dirt flew, the hole under the fence grew, and the sweat poured from both boys.

"We can't stop," said Joe, grunting with effort as he drove the blade of his shovel into the earth with all his strength. "Every minute counts. We have to take our chances and trust to luck."

"And if we run out of that, we have to trust to plan B," said Frank. "Let's hope we don't have to. We'd really need luck to get away with that one."

It took two hours of backbreaking work before the boys managed to dig under the fence. Then, leaving their shovels behind, they wiggled through on their stomachs. They were careful not to let their bodies touch the bottom of the fence. They didn't know what kind of alarm system might be in place.

"So far, so good," said Joe, brushing himself off.

"That was the easy part," said Frank. "Remember, keep down. Somebody might be on lookout."

They kept low to the ground as they made their

way toward the mansion, moving from bush to bush in the overgrown garden. They passed the spot where they had left Jacques and Henri. All that remained were two empty holes.

"I wonder how long they had to wait until somebody found them," whispered Frank.

"No matter how long, it couldn't have happened to two nicer guys," Joe whispered back.

By then the boys had reached the side of the clinic. They began to check the windows.

"Just as I figured, they're all locked," said Frank after they had worked their way around the mansion.

"The back door, too," said Joe. "Maybe we could break open one of the windows. We could throw in a rock wrapped with cloth to muffle the sound."

"Too risky," replied Frank. "This place is bound to be wired with alarms. We'll stick with the original plan. We'll go in through the front door."

Still hugging the side of the mansion, they moved to the large front door.

"Okay, you stand on one side, I'll stand on the other," said Frank. "We'll wait for somebody to come out, then jump him before he can close the door behind him. We'll tie him up and gag him, leave him in the bushes, and go in. After that, we'll do it your way. We'll play it by ear."

"All right. I'll try the door." Joe gave the big brass knob a turn, and the door swung open.

"Nothing beats helping yourself," he said, turning toward Frank to give him a triumphant grin.

But the look on Frank's face wiped his grin away.

He turned to find himself staring at Fritz and Hugo.

And at the assault rifles in their hands.

He didn't have to look at Frank again to know that plan A had just come to an abrupt end. It was time for plan B—fast.

"Hi, guys," he said to the Lazarus gunmen. "It's great to be back."

"Yeah, the job wasn't the snap it was supposed to be, not after those kids busted out of here and complicated things," Frank chimed in. Behind his back he dropped the coil of rope he was carrying. With an almost imperceptible motion of his foot, he shoved it under some shrubbery.

"Good thing we had a back-up plan," Joe added.

"Yeah, and it worked fine," said Frank. "We cooled the whole bunch of them."

Fritz and Hugo lowered their rifles.

"The boss will be glad to hear that," said Fritz. "He was getting a little worried—not hearing from you."

"There were some complications," Frank explained. "You know how it is. Even with the best-laid plans, little things can go wrong. Nothing important, though. We'll explain it all to the boss when we see him."

"See the boss, that's a laugh," said Fritz.

Frank remembered the voice of the Lazarus leader over the intercom—and his absence from view. "I mean, *talk* to him, of course."

"Yeah, like they say, take us to your leader," said Joe with what he hoped was a winning grin.

As Hugo and Fritz turned to lead them into the mansion, Frank and Joe exchanged quick nods. Then they moved.

Frank attacked Hugo from behind, and Joe attacked Fritz. Both Hardy boys used the same efficient punch on the back of the neck to knock the men out. Swiftly Frank retrieved the rope, and within minutes Fritz and Hugo were bound, gagged with their own shirts, and placed out of sight in a front hall closet.

"So far, so good," Joe remarked.

"Good?" exclaimed Frank. "We got through by the skin of our teeth."

"We've still got a crack at rescuing Iola," said Joe. "That's good enough for me."

"Now all we have to do is find her," Frank pointed out. Then his look of concern changed to a broad smile, and he said, "Hi, Ivan, how's it going? Broken any arms or legs lately?"

Ivan had emerged from a room off the hallway and stood staring at them. His mountainous body seemed to fill the doorway.

The Hardy boys didn't even have to look at each other to know what to do. Joe hit him low, with a tackle around the knees, and as Ivan bent over to grab Joe, Frank hit him high, with a chop that sent Boshevsky toppling over like a huge tree.

Then, muscles straining, the Hardy boys dragged his body back into the room from where he had come. They closed the door behind them.

"Looks like this is Ivan's workshop," said Frank, taking in the operating table complete with straps to hold down a victim.

"I think we can give big boy here a taste of his own medicine," said Joe.

With a mighty heave, Frank and Joe swung Ivan on the table and strapped him down.

"Time to wake up," said Joe, gently slapping the giant's cheeks until his eyelids flickered open.

"Talk and talk fast," said Frank. "Where is Iola?"

"You cannot get away with this," Ivan snarled, immediately realizing that his captors were the real Frank and Joe, and not Frank II and Joe II. "I will not say a word."

"I think you will," said Joe, and he let his gaze rest on a row of sharp metal instruments neatly laid out on a stand beside the operating table.

"She is in a room upstairs, on the second floor, the third door to your right," Ivan Boshevsky said quickly. "I am telling the truth, believe me. You don't have to—"

Frank cut off his speech with surgical tape he found next to the instruments.

"Never fails," he said to Joe. "The biggest bullies are always the biggest cowards."

Joe wasn't interested in philosophy. "Come on, let's move."

"Not so fast," said Frank. He opened the door to the room cautiously, and eased his head out. "Okay. The coast is clear. All systems go."

He and Joe ran up the stairway three steps at a time. Joe was the first to reach the door to which Ivan had directed them. Saying a silent prayer, he tried the knob. The door swung open.

Joe felt dizzy with joy when the girl sitting at a desk with her back to him turned around, and he saw that she was Iola.

"Joe, Frank, it is you, isn't it?" she cried, and the same joy lit her face. "This isn't another one of their tricks?"

"It's us all right," Joe said. "And we're getting you out of here."

"Oh, it's too good to be true," she said in a dazed voice. "How—?"

"We don't have time to explain it now," said Frank. "Let's hurry."

"Of course," Iola agreed, nodding. She stood up. "But before we go, let me just go get one thing."

"Iola, you haven't changed a bit," said Joe. "Every single time we were going to go out, you remembered something at the last minute and had to go back for it."

"That's right, I haven't changed at all," Iola replied, and opened a drawer in a table by her bed. "Well, maybe I've changed just a *little* bit. I didn't use to know how to use *this*."

Iola turned, a Luger pistol in her hand.

It was pointed straight at Joe's heart.

Chapter

14

JOE GRINNED. "HEY, Iola, watch where you're pointing that thing. It could go off. Remind me to teach you how to handle weapons sometime."

Iola didn't return his grin. And her weapon didn't waver. "You two do what I say. I don't want to have to use this. But one false move from either of you, and I will."

The voice was Iola's—yet it wasn't. Joe began to detect a mechanical sound to her words, as if they were being played on a tape.

"What's wrong with you, Iola?" asked Joe.

But Frank had already seen what Joe was unwilling to see. "We'd better do what she says, Joe. She means business with that gun."

"But—" Joe said.

"You have to face it," said Frank. "They've

succeeded in brainwashing her. They've made a puppet of her. She's in their hands."

"And right now you're in mine, and don't forget it," said Iola. Still covering them with her gun, she pressed a button on an intercom machine on her bedside table.

"What is it?" a voice answered.

At the sound of the voice, Frank and Joe exchanged glances. The voice seemed strangely familiar. It belonged to someone they knew, but who? The answer stayed maddeningly out of reach, even though both Hardy boys strained to come up with it as the conversation over the intercom continued.

"The Hardys busted in here, but I got the drop on them," said Iola. "What do you want me to do with them?"

"You're sure they're *the* Hardy boys and not *our* Hardy boys?" the voice replied, its tone charged with sudden alertness.

"I'm sure," Iola said. "Unless you were giving me some kind of test."

"Of course not. We have absolute confidence in you," said the voice. Then it paused, before going on, "That means something went wrong, very wrong, with plan B, after their escape fouled up plan A. We'll have to switch to plan C—the doomsday scenario."

"What's that?" asked Iola.

"You'll find out soon," the voice answered.

"Bring the boys to the conference room. I'll gather the others. It's time to wind things up here."

There was the click of the intercom being turned off, and Iola turned to the Hardy boys. "You heard the boss. Let's go."

"Is that your boss?" asked Frank. "You've had a change of leadership since we were here last. He sounds different."

"You'll see," was all Iola would say, and an impatient gesture with her gun stopped any more questions.

The conference room turned out to be the room where Frank and Joe had been questioned during their first visit to the clinic. Familiar faces greeted them when they entered.

There was the arrogant face of Dr. Helmut von Heissen, the impassive face of Colonel Chin Huan, and the pouting face of Peter Clark.

One more person was in the room. He was a man of average size and weight, wearing the same white lab coat as the others. But he was far different from them in one respect.

He had no face.

Or rather, his face was covered by bandages wrapped mummylike around his head, with gaps at the eyes, nose, and mouth.

But his voice identified him instantly. It was the voice that had spoken to Iola over the intercom. The Lazarus leader.

"I couldn't locate Fritz, Hugo, and Ivan," he said. "But I'm sure the Hardy boys here can tell us where they are."

"Talk," Iola ordered them.

Frank and Joe looked at the gun in her hand and then at the look in her eyes. Her pitiless gaze told them that her finger was tight on the trigger.

"Fritz and Hugo are tied up in the front hall closet," said Joe.

"And Ivan is strapped down in his torture chamber," added Frank.

"Get them," the Lazarus leader ordered his men. Von Heissen, Chin, and Peter Clark hurried off.

"We'll wait until everyone is assembled here," the leader said.

They didn't have long to wait. In less than ten minutes, the entire team was in the room.

"I wanted all of us to witness our latest triumph," the leader began proudly. "It will be good for our morale to see what achievements we are capable of—especially now, when we have suffered a slight setback. It will help inspire us in the period ahead, when we will have to suspend our operations until we find a secure new base."

He nodded to Dr. von Heissen. "My good Doctor, I will let you do the unveiling, since it is your superb skill we will be admiring."

"You do me a great honor," Dr. von Heissen said crisply. He removed a pair of surgical scissors from his worn black leather medical bag and,

130

with practiced expertise, snipped the bandages around the leader's head and carefully unwrapped them.

"It can't be!" exclaimed Joe, his jaw dropping.

"I knew that voice sounded familiar," said Frank, trying to remain cool and ignore the feeling that his brain was being scrambled.

Standing in front of them was the Gray Man.

"You see what a good job you did," the leader said to Dr. von Heissen.

"I must admit, I was a little worried," the doctor said. "Those snapshots I had to work from were not of the best quality, even though the Assassins claimed they were the best available."

"And your voice passed the test as well, Peter," the leader continued.

"It would have been even better if they'd given me better tapes," replied Peter Clark, his pale face flushed with pleasure.

"It is a shame that we could not get the information about this Mr. Gray that we needed from the Network head so that you could have programmed it into me, Colonel Chin," the leader told his chief brainwasher.

Chin shrugged. "Life is a balance of victory and defeat. One must accept both."

"I'm afraid we'll have need of your philosophy in the dark days ahead," said the leader.

By now Frank had stopped listening to the conversation. He was too busy trying to figure things out.

"So you planned on kidnapping the Network head and getting information from her about the Gray Man," he said to the Lazarus leader. "Then, after you were programmed well enough, you—" Frank paused, not wanting to say more. He suddenly felt a little sick.

"Very good," the leader said with a smile. "Please continue. I want to see how smart you really are."

"Yeah, go on," said Joe. "I'd like to make some sense out of all this, too."

"All right," replied Frank. "After you got the information you needed from the Network head, you planned to rub her out. Then you'd get your hands on the Gray Man, who was her natural successor. You'd rub him out, too, and take his place. And you'd be head of the most powerful undercover security force in America."

"Beautiful, isn't it?" said the leader. Then he shrugged. "Such a pity it didn't work out—this time. Dr. von Heissen will have to go to the trouble of giving me yet another face, for a while. I must decide if I want my old one, or a nice new one. I always did want to look like Robert Redford."

"Why not Count Dracula?" asked Joe. "It would be perfect for somebody who likes to suck the life out of the living." Angrily Joe looked at the Lazarus leader. Then he looked at Iola. She was still covering him with her pistol and looking at him with dead eyes. Joe could not believe what Lazarus had done to her.

The Lazarus leader smiled and turned to his team.

"I think we should let Joe in on the truth, don't you?" he said. "It is only fitting that he and his brother should appreciate how magnificent your work is, even though they might not applaud."

"What do you mean?" asked Joe, but Frank suspected what was coming.

"You tell them, Dr. von Heissen," ordered the leader.

"Iola here is one of my greatest successes," said Dr. von Heissen. "Of course, I had a great number of excellent photographs to work from. Iola's parents had a superb photo album of their late daughter."

"Their *late* daughter. But—" began Joe.

"See how astonished Joe is? How he still cannot believe this girl is not really his beloved Iola?" the Lazarus leader exclaimed. "And he knew her so well. Doctor, Colonel, Peter, your work has passed the ultimate test with flying colors."

"You can't kid me," said Joe. "Nobody but Iola could have known that stuff about all the times we were together by ourselves."

"There is one thing you did not know about Iola," said the Lazarus leader. "Your girlfriend kept a diary. An extremely detailed diary. It lay untouched in her room, along with her photo albums. All we had to do was get into her room while her parents were away, make copies, and use them to create the Iola you see before you, her looks, her voice, her memories absolutely true to life."

"But who are you?" Joe asked the girl in a stunned voice.

"I am . . . I am . . ." the girl paused and looked to her leader for help.

"Unfortunately, it was necessary to wipe out the memory of her previous identity to ensure total success in the transformation," said the leader. "Iola Two here only knows the part she is supposed to play, like an actress who has memorized her lines, and that she is to follow my orders without question. Am I right, my dear?"

"But you can't just make puppets out of people," Joe protested. "Human beings aren't made out of some kind of putty."

At that everyone except Iola II smiled—the leader, the team of scientists, and the two guards, all enjoying Joe's refusal to admit the truth of what he was seeing and hearing.

Iola II remained expressionless, her eyes blank, as she awaited orders.

Still smiling, the Lazarus leader said, "I see you are still not convinced, Joe. But maybe I can offer you final proof. I and the others are about to leave you alone with Iola, so that you will not be able to imagine she is acting out of fear of me. It would rob us of the full pleasure of our triumph if you were not totally convinced. Besides, I'm sure my scientific team here would welcome this excellent test of their work. It will prove valuable in future assignments."

The leader turned to Iola. "We are leaving now. I want you to wait fifteen minutes, then leave, too, and join us at the clearing in the forest. A helicopter will be waiting there to take us across the Canadian border to the hunting lodge."

Frank glanced at his watch to see what time the countdown was beginning.

The Lazarus leader caught the gesture.

"Are you in a hurry to go somewhere?" he asked Frank sarcastically.

"I'm just seeing how much time you have left," lied Frank, thinking fast. "The Network has this place surrounded. You might as well give up."

"You really expect me to believe that the Network would jeopardize an attack on the clinic by letting you try to rescue Iola?" The Lazarus leader laughed cruelly. "How amusing. The Network may be many things, but they are not fools. Nor am I. Your coming here could have only been inspired by something as idiotic as Joe's love for his girlfriend. I'm sure our young Romeo did not tell the Network our location. He wouldn't do anything to endanger his dear Iola."

"I wouldn't, but my double might have," said Joe. "I'm sure the Network has already made our doubles spill the beans about your location. You're not the only ones who play rough to make people talk."

"The Network can play as rough as they like with the doubles, but it will do them no good," said the leader. "Colonel Chin will tell you that."

"They are programmed not to reveal anything under any circumstances," Chin agreed.

"So you see, there is really nothing more to talk about—or to hope for," said the leader. He turned to his men. "Okay, let's get out of here."

But Iola stopped him. "Sir, you haven't told me what to do with the Hardy boys."

The Lazarus leader pretended to sound surprised. "Oh, didn't I? What an oversight. But I forgot, I can't leave it to your imagination, because you don't have one."

Then his voice hardened. "I'll tell you very simply what you are to do. After we leave, kill them, Iola. Kill them."

Chapter

15

THIS IS NOT Iola. This is not Iola.

Joe kept telling himself that as he looked at the girl who held him and Frank at gunpoint.

He saw her look at her watch. She must have been trying to decide exactly when she should squeeze the trigger. She would have to squeeze it just two times. No chance of her missing. The range was too close. Her gaze was too unwavering. Her gun hand was too steady. She was a machine perfectly programmed to kill.

And yet—

This is not Iola, Joe said to himself again.

The others must have left the house now. In a few minutes, it would be all over for the Hardy boys. In a few minutes, Iola—no, Iola II—would be running to join her leader and the others.

This is not Iola. But why then was the feeling

137

that surged through him the same as when he and Iola had been together? When Iola had been alive? When they had loved each other?

Joe remembered it all so clearly. He felt like a man seeing his life pass in front of him in his final seconds. He was seeing all the times he and Iola had shared. All the memories they had shared.

All the memories.

Suddenly Joe said, "Remember the time we went on that picnic and made plans to go to college together? Remember the way we kissed? Remember how we said we would never break up?"

Almost despite herself, Iola II replied, "Of course I remember."

"And remember the time we had that fight and we broke up? Remember how lousy we both felt? Remember how finally we both called each other at the same time and got busy signals and thought the other one was talking to somebody else? Remember how we laughed about it when we were back together again? Remember how wonderful it felt to be going steady again, after we thought we had lost each other forever?"

"And I gave you that ring and you gave me those earrings and we—" Iola II began. Then she paused, blinking her eyes, as if unsure where she was, in the present or the past.

By now Frank had realized what Joe was doing.

"I remember how great you two looked at the prom," he said. "In fact, I remember how great you looked all the time, whatever you were doing, whether you were walking or talking or sharing a pizza. It was like you weren't just going together, you *went* together. There was a kind of harmony between you. Everybody who knew you felt that. And you two felt it most of all. It was the kind of thing that happens between people just once in a lifetime maybe, if they're lucky. You have to remember that."

"Being together *was* special," Iola II agreed dreamily, looking into Joe's eyes. "I did love you so . . ."

"Why don't you give me that gun, Iola, before it goes off by accident," Joe said, extending his hand.

Iola II drew back. The gun, which had been drooping in her hand, steadied. "No, I can't. I'm supposed to—"

"Forget about that," Joe said. "I know you've got a conscience. Remember who you are, Iola. Remember who I am. Remember what we mean to each other."

"But I'm not—" Iola II began.

"How can you say that when you remember so clearly who you are, and how in love you and Joe were?" asked Frank.

"Right. Remember. All those times. All that love." Joe extended his hand again.

"But . . . I . . ." Iola II's voice, which had sounded confused, grew strong again. "But I do remember. How can I forget?"

She held the gun out to Joe, and as Joe closed his hand around the cold steel of the barrel and drew the weapon out of Iola II's unresisting hand, he felt a chill run through him.

It was as if Iola's love had come back from the grave to save him.

It was as if he stood in the presence of Iola's ghost.

Except that the girl in front of him was no ghost. She was very real and once again was very confused, not knowing who she was or what she was supposed to do. All she knew for sure was that the memories inside of her would not let her kill the boy she loved so much.

Joe and Frank exchanged glances.

"Those Lazarus people did quite a job," said Frank.

"Lucky thing they did," agreed Joe.

"I'd love to see the expressions on their faces when they find out how successful they were in planting all those memories," Frank went on.

"Maybe we'll get that chance," said Joe. "Maybe the Network will let us be in on the operation when they close in on the Lazarus group in Canada. Believe me, I'm going to ask for that favor."

"But first we have to get out of here fast,

before anyone gets suspicious about Iola not showing up," said Frank.

"You mean, Iola *Two* not showing up," Joe corrected him. He took the girl's arm and said, "Come on, Iola, we have to make a run for it."

"Whatever you say, Joe," she replied. "I know I can trust you."

"More than you can trust Lazarus," said Frank, who was already at the door. "This door is locked."

"But why—?" Iola II asked, more confused than ever.

"A better question is, how do we get out?" said Frank.

"Yeah," said Joe. "I've got a hunch it'd better be fast."

Frank examined the lock. "This is an old-fashioned model, probably put in by the original owner. There was no reason for Lazarus or the shrink who took over this place to change it, since the room wasn't meant to house patients or prisoners."

"We don't have much time," said Joe. "Stand aside, everybody."

Frank turned to see the Luger in Joe's hand. He followed orders.

"This might be crude, but it'll do the job," Joe said grimly, and blasted away the lock. He gave the door a shove. It swung open. Then he tossed the gun aside and led the others out of the room and into the deserted corridor.

"They've all gone, everyone but us," said Iola II. "This is so creepy, like a grave."

"Like a grave," agreed Frank, and then repeated in a sharper voice, *Like a grave.*" His tone became one of command. "Come on, let's run for it."

"What's the hurry? There's nobody to—" Iola II started to ask. But Joe had already grabbed her arm and was pulling her along as he broke into a run, following in his brother's flying footsteps.

They reached the front door.

Frank tried it.

"Good, they didn't bother to lock it," he said, and dashed out.

"They probably figured Iola wouldn't make it that far," said Joe as he and Iola followed.

They didn't stop running even when they were outside. They were thirty feet down the front path before they were stopped by a gigantic roar—and by a shock wave that sent them sprawling face forward onto the pebbles.

They felt a blast of heat on their backs, as, lying on their stomachs, they turned to see that the clinic had erupted in a mass of flames.

"The place exploded like a bomb," said Frank, after checking to see that Joe and Iola II had suffered no injuries other than the minor cuts and bruises that he had. He looked at his watch. Ten minutes had passed since the Lazarus group had left Iola II in the room to dispose of him and Joe. "Iola wasn't supposed to leave for five minutes yet."

"But they still locked the door in case she tried to leave early," said Joe. "Just like them."

"Typical," agreed Frank. "They always have a back-up plan."

"They wanted to kill me?" Iola II asked dazedly.

"They didn't need you anymore," replied Joe.

Iola II looked with horror at the sea of raging flames. Then her face hardened. "Those rats."

"Let's not get mad," said Joe. "Let's get even."

"Right," said Frank. "We'll find a telephone and try to contact the Network. We've blown the cover off the Lazarus criminals, and now, no matter how far they go, there'll be no place for them to hide."

"Are you in good enough shape to run a couple of miles?" Joe asked Iola II.

"I always could keep up with you," she answered, "or don't you remember?"

Joe looked at her, a lump forming in his throat. "I remember," he managed to say.

"Then let's do it," said Frank, and the three of them started running in easy strides. They ran through the front gate that had been left open by the fleeing Lazarus group and down the overgrown forest trail, dappled with sunlight filtering through the trees.

Suddenly Frank, Joe, and Iola II came to stumbling halts.

Frank had time for only one thought.

I should have figured it. They had one more back-up plan.

Stepping out of the trees to block their path was the Lazarus leader.

There was a big smile on his face.

And a big gun in his hand.

Chapter

16

INSTANTLY JOE KNEW what he had to do.

He charged straight into the barrel of the Lazarus leader's Smith and Wesson .38—a pistol that looked as big and as deadly as a cannon.

Joe didn't kid himself, though. He knew he didn't have a chance.

But he also didn't have a choice.

Maybe, just maybe, Frank could seize the advantage while Joe was being blown away.

It was worth trying, better than nothing. And their chances would be nothing if they surrendered.

Joe charged, waiting for the bullet to rip through him, wondering how bad the pain would be and how long it would last before it all ended.

But it didn't happen. Joe heard no pistol blast, felt no agonizing impact, as he covered the space between them, reached the Lazarus leader, slammed into him, and connected with a right cross that sent the leader staggering backward even as his mouth flopped open in an unsuccessful attempt to say something.

Suddenly men poured out of the forest, assault rifles in their hands. They surrounded Joe, Frank, and Iola.

"Sorry, I did my best," Joe said to the others. "But they've got a small army here."

Then, to his amazement, he saw Frank's face break into a giant grin.

"What's the joke?" Joe asked.

"Don't you see?" Frank answered maddeningly.

"See what? That we've had it? That Lazarus has won? I see all that okay," said Joe.

"Lazarus? You think these guys are from Lazarus?"

Joe took another look at the men surrounding them. This time he saw more than the rifles in their hands. He realized that none of them had been at the clinic. He saw that though they wore the outfits of deer hunters, their boots were highly polished. Two of them were helping up the man he had knocked to his feet, and the man was shaking his head groggily, then advancing on Joe with his hand out rather than his gun.

Joe's eyes widened. "Look, I'm sorry, I didn't know it was you," he said to the Gray Man.

"That's okay, Joe, it was an honest mistake. I

was thrown for a loss myself when we captured the Lazarus leader. He could have fooled me, if he hadn't been pretending to *be* me. In this game, there's no way you can tell the players without a scorecard."

"So you caught him and all the others?" asked Frank.

"Including the two who were piloting the helicopter," said the Gray Man. "A couple of French-Canadians."

"They wouldn't be called Jacques and Henri, by any chance?" said Joe.

The Gray Man nodded. "You know them?"

"We ran into each other," Joe replied.

"You'll be able to pump them for information about both Lazarus and the Assassins," said Frank.

"I assure you, we'll get everything they know out of them," said the Gray Man. "We have our methods."

"I guess you do," said Joe. "I've got to admit, I don't like some of them, but this time they sure came in handy." He laughed. "Lazarus was so confident there was no way you could get our doubles to talk."

"Actually, Lazarus was right," said the Gray Man. "We must find out their programming techniques. We could use them to make sure our own agents never break down. Those doubles wouldn't crack."

"Then how did you find us?" asked Frank.

147

"Child's play," replied the Gray Man, smiling. "All I needed to do was remember that the word *Lazarus* came up a couple of times during our little adventure in Washington. I fed that into our computer, along with the fact that you two had been on a fishing trip to Maine. The printout about the Lazarus Clinic appeared one minute later. Never underestimate the Network data bank. We've had this place totally surrounded for hours. In fact, we were just readying a full-scale assault when the Lazarus crew came running out, right into our arms."

"Glad they came out in time," said Joe. "Your attack might have been a little messy—for us."

The Gray Man cleared his throat. "Well, sometimes in our business, there are what we call unavoidable trade-offs. But of course, since you boys aren't professionals, you wouldn't understand."

Joe shot Frank a quick, triumphant glance. Then he said, "Oh, we understand, all right. Maybe that's why we're *not* professionals."

The Gray Man shrugged, the superior look on his face undisturbed. "I'm afraid you're not cut out for this kind of work. Still, I must admit that you've proved quite valuable."

"Can I ask a favor in return?" said Joe, a thought suddenly striking him. "Can I see the Lazarus leader one last time before you cart him away?"

"Sounds fair to me," the Gray Man answered.

"You come with me, Iola. This concerns you," Joe said to the girl, who stood beside him looking totally lost. Apparently, she had at last fully realized that she did not have a clue who she was or what she should do.

"What about me?" asked Frank. "Am I allowed to come, too?"

"As if I could keep you away from a mystery," said Joe.

The Lazarus leader, stripped down to his underclothes to avoid confusion with the Gray Man, was being held with his team under armed guard in a clearing. In the clearing, too, was the large helicopter that was supposed to fly them to safety.

"Tell me," Joe said to the leader. "Who is this girl? We have to give her back her real identity."

"And why should I tell you?" There was a look of pure hate in the eyes of the Lazarus leader. "You Hardy boys have ruined everything—my perfect plans, my great organization. All those years of work are down the drain."

"I'll give you one good reason to tell me," said Joe, and bunched his fist in front of the man's face.

"You can't stand by and let him threaten me like this," the Lazarus leader protested to the Gray Man, who was watching the exchange with a smile on his face.

"It would not upset me in the least to see your features rearranged," the Gray Man said.

149

"Talk fast," Joe ordered, cocking his fist.

"She was a high school student by the name of Sally Collins," said the Lazarus leader. "We needed a girl of Iola's size, and we found and kidnapped her. There was a newspaper story about her disappearance. Then there was a search, and then—nothing."

"At least we know who you are, Sally," Joe said to her.

"But what good will that do me now?" the girl cried. "I've got someone else's face and mind. I'm not Sally Collins; I'm not anybody."

"But *they* can do something about it," said Joe, indicating the Lazarus team. "If they destroyed Sally Collins, they can bring her back again." He turned to the Gray Man. "What do you think? Will you do that? Will you make *them* do that?"

"It's a brilliant idea, Joe," Frank said to his brother. He turned to the Gray Man. "You have to see how good it is. Not only can you use the Lazarus team to restore Sally's looks and memory, but you can make them change your double back to his original identity—unless of course you enjoy having two of you around, one good and the other evil."

"You kids come up with the craziest ideas," said the Gray Man, shaking his head in wonderment. "But I have to admit, this notion isn't bad. Especially since the Network might have a few other uses for these people as well. Yes, I can think of a number of situations in which they could be handy, under the proper supervision, of course."

"I hope I haven't created some kind of monster," Joe said.

"All's fair in the war against our enemies," the Gray Man said, his eyes gleaming at the thought of the new weapon in the Network arsenal.

"That's what I was afraid you'd say," replied Joe, and shrugged. He turned to the girl. "Anyway, Sally, you'll soon know who you are again."

She smiled gratefully at him. "Thank you, Joe." Then her smile faded. "But does that mean I won't remember anything that happened to me since I was changed?"

"I don't see how you could, or why you'd want to," Joe answered, wondering why she looked so concerned. "They'll probably arrange to have you found wandering around dazed, as if you had suffered some kind of blackout. Partial amnesia, I think they call it."

"Then I won't remember anything," she said, regret coloring her words. "I won't remember all that's happened between us."

"That's right," agreed Joe thickly. "It'll be all over. You won't be Iola anymore. Iola will be gone forever."

He looked at the girl and the girl looked at him. He felt as if a distance were already opening up between them.

The girl broke the silence. "Goodbye, Joe. And thanks for everything. I wish I could say I'll never forget you."

"Right." Joe was unable to continue speaking. He was losing Iola for the second time.

His fist clenched, he turned abruptly to the Lazarus leader. "Iola *is* gone, isn't she? Just as you said she was."

The Lazarus leader glared at him. "You'd like to know for sure, wouldn't you? You'd like to put your mind to rest, one way or the other. Well, I don't care if you beat me to a pulp, I'm not giving you your precious answer. Any pain you cause me will be only temporary—while I can leave you to agonize over your missing girlfriend forever."

Motionless, they faced each other. Then Joe unclenched his fist. "One-way fights aren't my thing," he said, and turned away. "But I'm not giving up," he told his brother. "Iola *is* alive, I can feel it. I couldn't feel this strongly about someone who was dead."

"Then I won't tell you to give up hope," Frank said softly. He put his hand on Joe's shoulder. "Anyway, solving mysteries is what we do best— and Iola is at the top of the list."

"You bet she is," said Joe, and he and Frank shook hands on that.

Frank and Joe's next case:

The Hardys are proud of Fenton Hardy's past as a New York City cop. But when an enemy from the old days turns up, Frank and Joe face a danger that could kill millions—starting with their kidnapped father!

Hidden bombs in the air conditioning systems of Manhattan skyscrapers are set to go off. The explosions will spread a deadly virus to everyone in the buildings. It's a monstrous revenge and a deadly challenge. Can Frank and Joe stop this plot and save their father? Find out in *Edge of Destruction*, Case #5 in The Hardy Boys Casefiles.